JEREMIAH

A STUD RANCH STANDALONE NOVEL

STASIA BLACK

Copyright © 2022 Stasia Black

ISBN 13: 978-1-63900-097-5

All rights reserved. No part of this publication may be reproduced, distributed, or transmitted in any form or by any means, including photocopying, recording, or other electronic or mechanical methods, without the prior written permission of the publisher, except in the case of brief quotations embodied in critical reviews and certain other noncommercial uses permitted by copyright law.

This is a work of fiction. Similarities to real people, places, or events are entirely coincidental.

NEWSLETTER SIGN-UP

Want to read an EXCLUSIVE, FREE novella, Indecent: a Taboo Proposal, that is available ONLY to my newsletter subscribers, along with news about upcoming releases, sales, exclusive giveaways, and more?

Get Indecent: a Taboo Proposal
https://geni.us/SBA-nw-cont

When Mia's boyfriend takes her out to her favorite restaurant on their six-year anniversary, she's expecting one kind of proposal. What she didn't expect was her boyfriend's longtime rival, Vaughn McBride, to show up and make a completely different sort of offer: all her boyfriend's debts will be wiped clear. The price?

One night with her.

1

Jeremiah

Sometimes I think if I just lived alone, life could be so simple. Yeah, yeah, when I needed to, I'd go find myself a hot, consenting woman to bury myself in...

I dropped a hand down and massaged myself through my jeans. Speaking of, it had been too fucking long. I paused right inside the barn door and stared out past the bunkhouse. The sun had just set, and the huge Texas sky was fucking on fire with pinks and neon oranges.

I shook my head, going back to my daydreams. Yep, alone, just me and the land. Me and the cows. They're dumb animals but usually kind-hearted enough once you get to know 'em.

At the end of the night, it'd be me and whatever I could rustle up for dinner while I listened to a podcast or two. Then maybe a book for the half hour afterwards I might manage to keep my eyes open before crashing into my mattress.

Then just enjoying the blessed dark of sleep till it was time to do it all over the next day.

God, it sounded like a good life.

I sighed, shook my head, and headed away from the ranch house, still only half rebuilt, and strode the twenty feet toward the bunkhouse with a brisk step.

The door opened from the other side before I could even put my hand on it.

"Where you been?" asked my twin brother, Reece, whose face was a perfect reflection of my own. "We been holding dinner." He dragged me in by an arm around my shoulder. "And listen, there's only about a thousand details of the wedding to go over. Charlie's been up my ass because Ruth's been up *her* ass wanting to know how many people are coming and need to be seated on our side of the aisle. And I had to tell her I didn't know 'cause you hadn't gotten back to me yet. You're my best man, bro. You gotta be on top of this shit."

I shook his arm off and nodded as I reached up into a cabinet for a glass so I could take a drink of water. My water bottle had gone dry an hour ago.

'Cause no. The universe did not give me silence, not from the very first moment I came into this world.

Well, they say I was born two minutes ahead of him.

So for two blessed minutes, there mighta been quiet. Or at least just the sound of my own voice howlin'.

But then—

"So, how many?" Reece asked. "Surely you've thought of a ballpark. You're *you*. You've probably already got it calculated ten ways from Sunday. I thought you said yesterday you were going to call Ruth and take care of it—"

"Can't a man get a goddamned drink?" I barked.

Reece held up his hands and looked toward Mike and Buck who were sitting around the kitchen table. "Touchy. Touchy. Who shit in your cornflakes today?"

I breathed out and spun away from him, turning on the sink water.

I will not punch my newly engaged brother, I chanted internally as I shoved the cup under the spout. *I will not punch my newly engaged brother. He's happy and I'm happy that he's happy.*

I yanked the water back and chugged it, gulp by gulp until the glass was empty.

"Look, the girls are up at the house," Reece kept at it. "They ate on the way over so they're doing some painting. I told them we'd be up there after dinner to help."

I was bone tired. I'd been up since five a.m. and hearing him talk only reminded me that the day was far from over.

But it wasn't the thought of having to take on this second shift—going to work on the big house after all the ranch work, since the contractors we'd hired were shit and about a month behind schedule. That meant we had to do a lot of the finishing touches ourselves on the downstairs, the only part of the house that *was* finished, and just section off the upstairs which didn't even have drywall up yet in some rooms.

No, my brain was stuck on the word *girls*.

"What do you mean—who's up at the house with Charlie?"

But I knew what he was gonna say even as he frowned at me. "Ruth."

I massaged my temple. I felt a headache coming on.

"What's your problem with her?" Reece asked. "We all lived in the same house for months and now it's like the two of you can't barely stand to be in the same room together."

I glared at my brother for stating the obvious. "I've had a long day. And that woman's mouth never turns off."

"Well, if Charlie's parents are coming in on Thursday, then we need all the help we can getting the place ready."

As if I needed another reminder of the circus about to come to town. I sat down at the table and spooned some of the taco meat piled in a bowl at the center of the table into a flour tortilla. There was only the meat, salsa, and a squeeze bottle of sour cream on the table in addition to the tortillas. Plus beer. Dinner of fuckin' champions.

"I thought Charlie hated her parents," I said, shoving a huge bite of taco into my mouth and chewing. "So why are we busting our asses to make 'em feel cozy?"

"They're paying for the wedding," Reece said, sounding exasperated. "I've told you a hundred times. This is a big deal for Charlie. She's sees it as a way to reconcile with them after everything that went down with her fucker of an ex."

I waved with my overstuffed taco. "Exactly. They took the side of that abusive fuck. So good riddance to 'em."

"It's not so easy to write family off," Mike piped up from across the table. "Even when they suck." I looked over at him where he was sopping up the bits that had fallen out of his taco with the last of his tortilla. Beside him, Buck was playing an obnoxiously loud game on his phone, ignoring all of us.

I shook my head. "Seems pretty cut and dried to me. They abandoned her when she needed them." I sliced the hand not holding my taco through the air. "They made their choice."

But Reece just shook his head. "You know Charlie's not like that. She's got a big heart and she feels like if they're willing to come halfway, she wants to meet them there."

I rolled my eyes. Whatever. From what I'd seen, and I'd seen a fucking lot, people never changed.

We finished up dinner and then headed over to the big house. The insurance money from the tornado had all gone to Ruth since she'd still owned the quarter acre the damn house was on, in a nasty little bit of fine print she'd squirreled past our boss Xavier's lawyer. But at least she'd finally sold it to him, so now he owned the entire ranch outright. But it meant he'd also had to shell out the cash on an already huge investment for the house rebuild.

So we tried to keep costs down where we could, including going with the lowest bidding contractors—a mistake, and one that had been my decision.

Xavier had given me this project and I'd yet to prove much of anything in the way of leadership skills. Selling the first calves two weeks ago had helped even out the ledger books, but we were still operating in the red.

So Reece and I were finishing up what work on the house we couldn't contract out.

As we walked up, Charlie stepped out the front door. Her short hair had grown out from being nearly bald like when she first arrived, but she still kept it shortish and dyed pitch black, like a little goth pixie.

"Babe!" Her face lit up at seeing Reece and she threw her arms around him. "Ruth got the caterer we wanted. They had a last-minute cancellation and we got them!"

Reece grinned big. He lifted her up off her feet and I had to give it to the bastard. He really did look happier than I'd ever seen him. He and Charlie had taken forever to actually start dating and admit that they liked each other for real. But once they did, it was a damn whirlwind. Of course, it was with my impatient brother. He was proposing by their three-month anniversary.

I told him it was too fast, that she'd just gotten out of a shit marriage and the last thing she probably wanted was to be saddled with another man's ring on her finger, but what the fuck did I know?

Reece proposed anyway and she said yes and the two of them have never looked fucking happier.

And frankly, I don't know why the whole thing's put me in such a bad damn mood.

When Reece finally set her down on her feet, she was pulling her phone out of her jeans pocket.

"But Ruth says we need to decide like, tonight, between the type of meat dish we want to serve." She started flipping through options on her phone and Reece zeroed in like he was studying for a math exam.

I just shook my head and pushed past the both of them. "I'll be inside."

I only realized my mistake once I opened the door and heard the sounds of Britney Spears' tinny voice and saw Ruth Harshbarger shimmying her backside while she rolled a roller of grey paint sloppily up and down the wall.

The door shut behind me with a loud enough bang, but the

music was so loud she didn't notice and kept dancing back and forth while visible paint flecks flew off the roller in all directions.

And I took in several things at once:

One, the way she was dancing was pulling up the plastic that she'd only haphazardly laid over the newly installed carpet.

Two, she was painting the walls but the ceiling was still naked drywall.

And three and most annoying of all, her ass looked fan-fucking-tastic in those paint-smeared leggings that did absolutely nothing to hide the shapely contours of each of her plump globes and Jesus fuck, it had been *way* too long since I'd been laid.

"What the hell are you doing?" I barked.

Ruth shrieked and turned around, finally noticing me. As she did, her foot banged into a can of paint, knocking it over.

It spilled onto the plastic—and over the edge onto the carpet.

"Son of a bitch," I yelled, leaping forward to try to rescue the situation. At the same time Ruth gasped and dropped to her knees.

She was trying to shove the paint back into the can with her hand, a completely fucking useless gesture at this point.

"Get out of the way," I said, shouldering in as I dropped to my knees, trying to grasp the edges of the plastic to lift it, but it was too late. The paint had overflowed onto the carpet in a gush of gray goo.

Ruth's eyes flashed at me, and at the same time, we both yelled, "Look at what you did!"

"What *I* did?" I scoffed. "You're the one painting with an open can of paint right at your feet."

Her mouth dropped open. "I was doing just fine until you came in and scared the shit out of me."

"Doing just fine?" I laughed. "You were painting the goddamned *walls* without painting the ceiling first."

"What?" she spat. "You don't paint ceilings." Then she looked up. And blinked.

"Yeah, you do, genius. What the hell else do you think you do to them?"

"I don't know." She looked flustered. "I've never painted ceilings before."

I looked at the splotchy wall. "Because you've done *so* much painting in your life."

She stood up and backed away, finally. I scooped up the plastic, containing as much of the paint spill disaster as I could.

"Oh, pardon, I was just trying to help *your* ass out," she said. "This isn't even my house anymore."

I glared up at her, arms full of plastic, paint oozing out onto my shirt as I strode toward the front door. "And thank fucking Christ the tornado took care of that at least."

"You better run," she called after me, sounding furious, "otherwise I'd kick you in the balls for saying that!"

I slammed out the front door, startling Reece and Charlie who were still in a cozy tete-a-tete over her phone.

Reece's eyebrows hit his hairline. "You were only in there like three minutes. How the hell did you two piss each other off that fast?"

2

Ruth

"Why does the man you fell in love with have to be related to that oaf?" I asked as I jammed my truck into drive, spitting gravel as I sped away from the ranch I'd grown up on. Every time I came back here my heart ached because I knew there'd be this moment when I'd have to drive away again.

Because it wasn't mine anymore. Dad had made sure of that with his gambling and terrible management, driving us into debt so that when he'd died, I'd had no choice but to sell.

Even with the insurance money from the tornado, I'd only finally been able to pay off some more creditors who'd came out of the woodwork at the news of my so-called "big payday."

Charlie sighed and I felt bad. I knew she was stressed to the max and she didn't need my petty bullshit with her fiancé's twin added to it.

"Sorry," I hurried to say. "Don't worry, we'll play nice."

"I didn't realize about the ceilings anyway. He shouldn't have gotten mad at you. I'll tell Reece to talk to him."

I waved a hand, eyes on the narrow gravel road leading out of the ranch to the main road. It was dark and deer roamed all about these parts after nightfall. "No, seriously. You've got enough on your plate."

"So do you. I know it was a big ask for you to take on all the wedding planning."

I shook my head. "Come on. We both know you did me a favor throwing this gig my way."

"Well, if Mom wants to buy my love by spending sixty thousand dollars on a wedding, it only makes sense to send some of that my best friend's way."

I rolled my eyes, glad for the dark. From everything Charlie had told me about her mother, the woman sounded like a piece of work, but it was true enough about the money. And I'd lived in the area long enough to know a lot of vendors, so I was *mostly* confident I could do the job. Since I'd paid off all Dad's debt, I was back in good standing with the community at least. People accepted that Dad was a fuck-up, but they'd finally stopped taking it out on me.

And with the money from this and the little bit I'd been able to squirrel aside from the house insurance money, hopefully I'd be able to put a down-payment on a place of my own and really start over.

First, we all just had to survive this wedding.

"So is the carpet for sure ruined?" I asked as we finally pulled onto the backroads that would take us back to Austin and the little apartment we shared there. Charlie didn't know it yet, but I'd be leaving just a few weeks from now too. I hadn't renewed the lease after all.

I'd had a job offer in Fort Worth; a job actually related to my degree that actually paid real money. But I hadn't had the heart to tell Charlie yet. Not before her wedding. I'd tell her when she got back from her honeymoon, I told myself.

Charlie hesitated then answered. "Yeah, the guys were pulling the carpet up right as I was leaving. It was ruined."

Dammit!

"But it was probably gonna get screwed up one way or the other. It was really those dumb contractors' fault for putting down carpet before painting, anyway. Everyone knows that you work from the top down."

"Starting with the ceiling, apparently," I said sourly.

Charlie threw her hands up. "Well, what are we supposed to know about finishing up house construction! I knew painting needed to happen so I offered and said we could help. No one told me to start with the ceilings."

My fingers tightened on the wheel as she continued, "Reece said he thinks they can put down some planking that looks like hardwood instead of carpet anyway. So it will turn out better in the long run."

"And how long will that take? It's Sunday and your parents get in on Thursday. We need to get it decorated and make it comfortable for them. There still isn't even a toilet installed in the ensuite. From what you've told me, they aren't going to be comfortable running out to the bunkhouse to take a shit."

Charlie busted out laughing and then clapped a hand over her mouth. "Jesus, it's not funny. But the thought of my mom running into Buck in the middle of the night—" She started laughing again. "Reece said he lives up to his name and the dude sleeps buck naked."

We both cringed in unison. Then I looked over at her and grinned. "Well, it would definitely make her appreciate that Reece was the cowboy you chose to fall in love with. At least he's cute."

But that only had her eyebrow lifting. "Oh yeah? So that means you still think Jeremiah's cute too?"

I made a gagging noise. "Ugh, no, God. I regret ever telling you that I ever—" I shook my head, then shook my whole body. "No. Absolutely not. *Never*."

When Charlie was silent, I looked over at her again. She just had one eyebrow lifted.

"Don't look at me like that. Yes, when we all lived together, I might have *briefly* had a proximity-to-male-hormone-induced madness that made me briefly consider—and I do mean only briefly *consider*—taking him as a lover. But it was only ever to get the itch out of my system. And I assure you, continued exposure to him has cured me of it."

She was still quiet until I glared at her and she lifted her hands. "Okay, okay. If you say so."

"Good. Because I do."

"Hey, that's my line."

"Ha ha." I rolled my eyes at her. "You are so cheesy. Reece is rubbing off on you."

"I know," she said, sighing happily. If she didn't sound so genuinely damn happy, I would've gagged. She'd dealt with her load of terrible, so I wouldn't begrudge her finding herself an actual good guy.

Even if he did happen to have an evil twin.

"I don't have time for a man right now, anyway," I said. "I've got this wedding to pull off and..." I trailed off momentarily before finishing strong, "a house that's just my own to find."

"That's right, cause my girl's gonna take over the *world*!"

"Hell yeah, I am. We both are!"

And then I turned on the radio and cranked it up as we sang along at the top of our lungs.

3

Ruth

I was feeling less enthusiastic and optimistic the next day as I stood on the side of the road glaring down at my phone and sweating out every single particle of water in my body under the scorching Texas sun.

It was just my luck that I ran out of gas on *today* of all days. And that lever on the gas indicator had just bottomed out outta freaking nowhere. I'd swear I just glanced at it and it had been at a fourth of a tank!

Granted, that glance might have been yesterday... before I'd driven Charlie and me over to the ranch and back, but *still*. Back in the day Betty woulda been able to get me twice that distance on a fourth of a tank.

I held a hand over my eyes and glared down the road, then grabbed the door to the truck and climbed back inside if only to get out of the sun. It was hotter than an oven in the fires of hell inside, though, even with all the windows down. It was supposed to rain later today—a big storm, but it hadn't swept in yet.

Why the hell hadn't I gotten on a bus and ridden out of this town the moment that tornado swept my family's house away, I'd never know.

I was in the hill country and cars passed, some even slowed, but I waved them by. I'd called Charlie and she was coming by with gas.

But when the familiar truck slowed down to a stop behind me and a lanky figure climbed out, it definitely wasn't Charlie. By his rigid posture and the permanent stick up his ass, I knew it wasn't Reece either.

I got back out of my car, hands on my hips. "Why'd they send you?" I glared at Jeremiah as he pulled out a gas can from the box in the back of his truck bed.

His eyes narrowed. "Oh, believe me, I have better things to be doing than rescuing you."

"Rescu—" The gall of this guy. "Well, give me the gas and your chivalrous act for the decade can be over and done with." I reached forward and tried to grab the gas can out of his hand, but he wouldn't budge.

"Why don't you just sit back and let me take care of it. Considering what happened with the paint can last night, I'd hate for this gas to accidentally end up all over the ground instead of in your tank."

I crossed my arms over my chest. "Did you have to go to jackass school or does all this charm just come natural?"

He shook his head as if I was the one being childish. God, I wanted to grab him and just shake all his superiority out of him. But I guessed the quicker he got the gas in my engine, the sooner I'd be done with him. So I stepped back and let him open my gas cap, align the nozzle, and upend the can.

"This isn't much, but there's a station a couple miles down the road. You'll need to stop there and fill up all the way."

"I know," I said. God, did he think I was an idiot?

"And you should keep a better watch on your tank. It's best to always refill when you hit a fourth of a tank, otherwise sediment from the gas can start to build up at the bottom of the—"

"Thanks, Mansplainer, I got it," I said as the noise of the gas *glug glugging* finished and I could finally yank the gas can out of his hands and roll my gas cap back on. "You can go now."

But he just stood there. "Let's just make sure she starts up."

I rolled my eyes but shoved the gas can back toward his chest. He took it and I climbed up into the truck's cab and shoved the keys inside.

I turned the keys and the engine sputtered. But didn't catch. What the—

I pressed the gas a little and then turned the keys again. Another sputter. And still nothing.

"Goddammit!" I slammed the wheel, glancing at the clock on the dash. I was already late for dropping off the deposits I'd promised would be in by four o'clock today. Shit.

"Pop the hood," Jeremiah said, sounding annoyingly calm.

It showed my level of desperation that I actually did what he said. Through my front windshield I saw him walk around the car and lift the hood, propping it open. I pushed out of the car and walked around to join him under the sweltering sun as he looked down at my engine.

It looked like... well, an engine. Nothing was smoking or giving away what was wrong. I looked at Jeremiah and he had a frown on his face. "Well?" I asked.

He shrugged. "No clue."

I huffed out a laugh at that. So Mr. Great and Mighty didn't know everything. But my mirth was quickly covered by panic.

"Shit. I have to get these deposits put down today. It's the last day to drop off Benny's check or else no booze."

Beside me, Jeremiah huffed out a noise of frustration. "Fine. I'll take you."

I looked up at him in surprise. "You will?"

Jeremiah pulled out the rod keeping the hood up and let it slam closed. "This piece of junk isn't taking you anywhere. And I have a feeling this wedding is gonna need all the social lubrication it can get."

Did he really just say *lubrication*? *Shit, get your brain out of the gutter, Ruth.* I shook it off and nodded. "Okay, sure. If it's not too far out of your way."

He just waved a hand, as gracious about it as I suppose he was able, because he still looked as disgruntled as a goat. "You should call for a tow. Don't expect me chauffeuring you around town to become a regular occurrence. Only reason I'm out here instead of Charlie or Reece is cause I need some materials in town and they thought I could hit two birds with one stone."

"What are they doin'?"

Jeremiah grimaced as I locked up my truck and followed him back to his. "They were eating lunch and planning some sort of wedding crap. Vows or some shit. I was about to head out anyway when Charlie got your text."

That made sense. God knew he'd never volunteer to come out and help me all on his own.

"All right, where to first?" he asked once I'd climbed up inside his truck. I looked over at him and would swear this truck cab had looked way bigger from the outside than inside. He was peering out the front windshield. "Clouds are comin' in so we better hurry."

I nodded absentmindedly. But now that I was closed up in here with him, breathing the same co-mingled air—I immediately turned away from him and glared out the window, shifting in my seat.

"So..." I said to the window, trying to calm my suddenly unsteady breathing. "To Benny's?"

"Right. The liquor." I could feel him nod even though I wasn't looking at him. In fact, I could feel every movement of his big body on the long seat we shared as he shifted the truck into gear—it was a manual, naturally.

The truck engine was loud as we got going, but it was still too quiet in the cab of the truck. I could hear Jeremiah breathing. I turned and reached toward the radio only for my hand to run into Jeremiah's, who'd apparently been reaching for the radio at the same time.

I yanked back and he glanced over at me, surprised.

"Oh," I said, then felt stupid. Especially when he didn't pause for a second in turning on the radio to some old country station. And by old, I mean *old*. Hank Williams Sr. old.

"You have *got* to be kidding me."

"What?" Jeremiah glanced my way.

I just shook my head and reached for the dial. His big hand blocked me, though. "No way. My ride, my tunes."

"Oh my God, you really are an old man in a young body."

"You checking out my body?"

My mouth dropped open and furiously, I felt my cheeks heat. "You wish. I'm not *that* hard up." I crossed my arms over my chest. But then, frustrated, I reached over and snapped the dial of the radio off. Better silence than having my ears assaulted like that.

Wisely, he didn't say anything else. But minutes later I was second-guessing turning off the music. Maybe ancient old white man hollering about his dogs was better than being painfully aware of every movement and twitch of the man on the seat beside me. Especially since on these backwoods roads, he was constantly reaching for the long shifter between us, nearly grazing my thigh each time. My bare thigh.

Jesus, maybe I'd been lying. Maybe I *was* hard up. It was true I hadn't had sex for a good long while. It was almost a year now. But considering the train wreck that some of my past relationships had been, I wasn't exactly racing to find the next Mr. Right Now.

Thankfully, we pulled into Benny's and I all but exploded out of the car as soon as it came to a stop. I expected Jeremiah to stay in the car, but a tall shadow was blocking the last of the sunlight as the clouds rolled in as I reached for the door. A raindrop splashed my cheek.

I spun on him and glared. "I'm just dropping off a check. I don't need babysitting."

His face was a placid mask. "I'm hungry. They have good burgers."

"I don't have time to stop and eat! We still have to go by the dress shop and then to get over to Wimberly to put in the check for the caterers."

His features didn't change. "Then I guess you shoulda checked your gas gauge before you left this morning."

Ugh, he was impossible. I shook my head at him and then stormed inside. He was right on my heels.

By the time I'd gone to the back and dropped off the check with Maria, Benny's partner, Jeremiah had installed himself on a barstool and his eyes were glued to the game playing on the TV up in the corner. I crossed my arms and tapped my foot impatiently. Eventually, his eyes came my way. "You tappin' away like that isn't gonna make George cook any faster."

I smiled at him hard. "I don't know, I think it just might." I started tapping louder and more obnoxiously. The rain outside began to *ping ping ping* on the tin awning of the entryway as the gentle shower became a downpour outside.

For a few minutes, he ignored me. The bar was pretty empty except for us. So I knew he could hear me. Confirmed when he finally turned to me, eyes flashing. "If I'm an old man, then you've been possessed by the demon of a goddamned *child* who doesn't know how to sit still."

I grinned even wider, delighted to have gotten under his skin. I had no clue why it felt like such a victory. "Aww, is someone having a grouchy day? You know, if you frown too much, your face will get stuck that way."

"Fine by me. I never give a shit what people say about me."

I think he even meant it. Which was infuriating. Everyone in a small town was conditioned to care what other folks thought about you. Gossip was our bread and butter, occasionally even our currency.

When Maria brought out Jeremiah's burger a few minutes later, it wasn't in a to-go box. When I made an exasperated noise, he just looked my direction and picked up his burger. "It'll take me five minutes to eat it. Five minutes ain't gonna kill any dead things."

I rolled my eyes. "Oh, fine," I said and reached over to snatch a hot, salty fry. And then another.

"Get your own," Jeremiah said with his mouth full, yanking his plate away.

"I've barely eaten today and you've got a plateful."

"Kitchen's open." He gestured toward the menu plastered on the wall. "No one's stopping you."

I crossed my arms over my chest. "No, I'm fine. I'll just wait and eat after we're done with our errands like I'd planned."

"Suit yourself." He shoved another huge bite of burger in his mouth. He'd already downed almost half of it in two bites. He really would be done in five minutes. Still, any gentleman would've shared his fries.

Ha. Who was I kidding. Jeremiah Walker? A gentleman?

"Oh, fine," he sighed. "If you're gonna make eyes about it." He shoved his plate back toward me.

I grinned and grabbed two fries, dipping them in the little bowl of ketchup at the edge of his plate.

We finished off the food and then headed out, covering our heads and dashing to the truck through the rain. We stopped off at the dress shop and then got to the caterers *right* before they closed—but at least I'd made it and the last check was delivered.

I climbed back up into the cab, slightly damp, and breathed out in relief. "All done."

"Good," Jeremiah said, "Cause I told Raul I'd be by his ranch before sunset to pick up the horse trailer I just bought off him."

"Why do you need a—"

"It's my boss's wedding present for Reece. He's driving a gelding down with him when he and his family come. And I'm buying a roan off him. Always meant to have horses around the place."

I nodded. I guess I'd known they were fixing up the stables. There just hadn't been horses on the HB Ranch for over a decade. Not since I was a kid. I had a horse named Winnie till I was eleven and we had to sell her cause we couldn't afford her upkeep. It was stupid that it made me swallow down a lump in my throat even thinking about it after all this time.

"Cool," I said, looking out the passenger seat window.

The views were spectacular as we crested hill after hill and the vista of the entire valley was spread out before us. I tried to enjoy the view since for once I wasn't driving.

The rain got harder though, really driving, and soon there wasn't much to see. There were a couple rainy seasons in Texas—the usual one, spring, and then again in fall sometimes during hurricane season, when any came through the Gulf Coast. I thought I remembered them talking about a tropical depression or something on the news this morning. I hadn't paid much attention because it'd been downgraded from a hurricane and it wasn't landing during the actual wedding.

I religiously stalked the ten-day forecast and while there were supposed to be showers late today, the furthest of the ten day was still clear with sunny skies, thank God.

When the road dipped down to cross one of the many streams that was usually a trickle, if not bone dry by this time of year, there was water rushing underneath the bridge.

Jeremiah grimaced as he slowed the truck down. "I don't like the look of that."

"How much farther is it?"

"Another twenty minutes."

I pushed up so I could look over my shoulder at the stream. It was still about two feet below the road but I'd lived in the area long enough to know how quick flash-flooding could hit with rain like this. At the same time, we were on a tight schedule. It wasn't like Jeremiah had another half day to waste coming all the way back out here.

I looked back at Jeremiah. "If we're quick it should be fine."

He nodded and we kept on going forward.

When we came to another low water crossing—I wasn't sure if it was the same stream curving back around again or a different one—I looked to Jeremiah, expecting him to second-guess the decision to keep going forward. But he didn't even slow down this time. He barreled on ahead; if anything, stepping on the gas even more.

Okay. Well, apparently, we were doing this.

I held onto the door as the truck bounced along the uneven road and we climbed back up another hill out of the valley.

Raul's place was at the top of a twisty hill, the dirt road turned to mud. A vehicle without four-wheel drive wouldn't have been able to even make it to the top. Jeremiah's jaw was locked as he maneuvered the truck the last bit to the top, slipping and sliding as the wheels fought the mud for traction, but finally getting us there.

I was tempted to stay in the car while Jeremiah did his business, but my Texan blood wouldn't let me. Plus the fact that considering the conditions out there, I was damn well gonna make sure he attached the trailer correctly.

So as soon as I saw Jeremiah and another man—Raul, I assumed—line up the trailer, I jumped out to go watch as they hitched it. I was drenched in two seconds from the pouring rain, but that was nothing new.

They were just attaching the chains, two, which was regulation, and they'd gotten the ball and lynch pin on right.

Jeremiah waved me away and I went back to the car after a quick look at the trailer. It wasn't new by any stretch of the imagination. I hoped Jeremiah hadn't paid much for it. That it was "functional" was the best that could be said for it.

Rain dripped from my hair onto my face and I cranked up the heat, but only for a second, because that quickly made it feel too humid and stuffy.

Minutes later I felt a tug on the truck like they were testing the chains, then Jeremiah was yanking open the door and jumping back in the driver's seat.

"All right, let's get the hell outta here."

I nodded. Fine by me.

It took some maneuvering to turn around in the tight space of the parking area by Raul's ranch house, especially in the mud, but we finally made it and then we were trundling back down the hillside.

I could tell Jeremiah was trying to take it slow and careful, but with the added weight of the trailer behind us, it was occasionally just a controlled slide. I think we were both breathing easier once we made it back to the pavement of the main county road. My knuckles were white from clutching my door and the oh shit bar, anyway.

It was still about an hour till we got back home, but at least we were off that damn hill.

I was feeling better, till we got to the first low-water crossing, anyway. And saw that the water had somehow gained the two feet in the forty-five minutes it had taken us driving and hitching the trailer.

"Jesus," Jeremiah swore, driving over the barely dry road. I plastered my face to the window, watching as the water started sloshing at the sides of the bridge, threating to come over. It would, any moment. We were only just making it in time.

I didn't say anything, tense until we'd made it across the other side. I only glanced Jeremiah's way once we were across. His jaw was tense again and I wondered if he was thinking the same thing I was.

We still had another crossing to go.

And the rain wasn't letting up, not one bit.

It was getting dark out, even though theoretically it was still an hour from sunset. The clouds overhead just made it so dark.

And then we came up to the second crossing. At first, I thought it was fine. But once the headlights of the truck flashed over the road in full, I saw that what I'd at first mistaken for the dark of the asphalt on the bridge was actually a mirage—because there was at least three inches of dark brown water flowing right over top of it.

"Dammit!" Jeremiah slammed the brakes and then smacked the wheel with the palm of his hand.

I was tempted to say we should try and drive over it anyway, but I'd lived here long enough to know better. It only took a couple inches to make you hydroplane and I'd seen cars washed over bridges in less water than this.

"If we turn back, we could still get over the other bridge and find another way around," I said, looking over my shoulder.

"Turn around, how exactly?" Jeremiah turned to me, clearly pissed. "There's no shoulder and we've got a trailer."

"I don't know!" I threw my hands up. "A three-point turn? Or a thirty-point turn, whatever it takes."

He shook his head. "There's no point. By the time we get back to the other crossing, it'll be flooded too."

I made an exasperated noise. "We have to try. We can't just stay here."

He gave me a side-long look. "Oh yes, we can."

My mouth dropped open. "And if the water keeps rising?"

"I'll back up some. It's higher ground here, and unless the river rises another ten, fifteen feet, we'll be fine."

Was he joking?

Apparently not, because he put the truck in reverse, and actually managed to back up in a straight line even with the trailer attached. It might've impressed me if he wasn't suggesting we just—what? Stay here until when? Until the water went back down again? That could be—

I made another exasperated noise. "We can't just stay here! We don't have any food or water."

Jeremiah just reached across my lap to the dash. I withdrew in distaste from his close proximity as he rustled around and pulled out two half-crushed granola bars. He tossed one in my lap. Then he reached behind his seat and pulled out two empty water bottles. I jumped as he shoved his door open, the driving rain assaulting my ears after the relative quiet inside the cab.

I watched through the back window as he set the two bottles in the back of the truck bed, wide-lipped tops off. He propped the bottles upright between some tools he pulled out of his truck box. I could see rainwater splashing inside the clear plastic bottles, filling a fourth of an inch at the bottom of them already.

God, he was annoying when he went all MacGyver like that. I ripped the bar on my lap open and shoved a huge bite in my mouth.

It was a little stale but still, food was food, and I really hadn't eaten anything beside the fries Jeremiah had spared me during lunch. Was I wishing I'd taken the time to order a fat, juicy burger like he had? Yes, yes, I was.

I was also wishing I hadn't gotten out back at Raul's because now I was stuck in these wet clothes for God knew how long. I shifted and my butt squelched on the truck seat. I grimaced. Dear God, was I really stuck here? Cold, wet, hungry, and with—?

"There," Jeremiah announced, freshly doused with rainwater as he got back up into the cab, all but shaking his hair like a dog does when it's wet.

I held up a hand. "God, please. Some of us are trying to get dry."

"Oh, I'm sorry, Princess. Was me trying to get you some water to drink so you don't get dehydrated making you uncomfortable? I guess her majesty will have to get out and get her own water from now on."

"Don't be a jackass. You know that's not what I meant."

"Do I?"

I rolled my eyes. He was determined to be impossible. I shoved another bite of the granola bar into my mouth, not taking the bait.

But the silence in the cab with only the rain continuing to pelt the front windshield quickly grew unnerving.

"So what now?" I asked as soon as I'd swallowed.

"Now we wait." He turned off the truck and stretched his legs out —well, as much as he could considering he couldn't exactly lean his seat back very far before bumping into the back of the truck. And his legs were too dang long to stretch out straight. He grabbed his cowboy hat off the seat between us and settled it low over his head so it covered his eyes.

"You're going to take a nap? Seriously?"

"Don't see what else there is to do. Seems like a fine idea to me."

I made an exasperated noise. "We're both wet to the bone and stuck in the middle of nowhere and taking a *nap* is your answer?"

He gave a long-suffering sigh and tipped his hat back so he could look at me. "And what exactly do *you* think we should do."

I lifted my cell phone. "Uh, how about we call for help?"

Jeremiah just nodded toward the low-water crossing. "And who exactly do you think is gonna be able to cross that and rescue us?"

"I don't know. A firetruck?"

He scoffed. "We aren't in danger and it's hardly an emergency. You wanna waste taxpayers' hard-earned money just cause you don't want to spend an uncomfortable night in a truck?"

Spend the *night*? He thought we'd be here all night? But looking at the water that seemed several inches higher already rushing over the road... dammit, he was right.

"Plus, they might just tell us to stay put anyway—I'm not sure a rig could make it across that any better than we could."

"And if it keeps rising? What if we *do* get in real danger and we could've been saved if we'd only called earlier?" I shook my head at him and started dialing for help... except I had no bars. A frequent problem out here in the nooks and crannies of the hill country. "Dammit! Give me your phone."

He reached in the pocket of his jeans, which were cemented to his lean legs by the rain and pulled out his phone. But his was the same. No service. "Ugh," I said in frustration, handing it back to him.

"Like I said," he settled his hat back over his eyes. "We wait."

How was he so damn calm about all this? I wasn't good with sitting still. I felt like I wanted to crawl out of my skin being stuck in the small space. It wasn't that I was claustrophobic exactly... I just preferred open space where I could move and see the big wide-open sky overhead—and not have a big male body beside me breathing so loud and suffocating all the available air.

I pulled my phone back out and tapped on Solitaire. Thank God I at least had a few games already downloaded that I could play offline.

But an hour later the phone had beat me more times than I'd beaten it, and as far as I could tell, Jeremiah wasn't even sleeping as often as he was shifting like he couldn't get comfortable. And still, the rain hadn't let up.

"This is ridiculous," I said, slamming my phone down on the seat between us. "I'm going to go out of my mind with boredom. At least talk to me so I don't go freaking nuts."

At first, he didn't react, but finally, he tipped his hat back, exposing his long-suffering facial features as he looked my way. "Fine. What do you want to talk about?"

"I don't know—just talk. Like normal people do. You don't have to make it awkward."

"Wow, you make such an inviting proposition. No thanks, I think I'll keep napping."

I snatched the brim of his hat and yanked it away before he could resettle it over his face. "Oh cut the bullshit, you aren't even sleeping."

He glared my way. "Has any one ever told you that you are the most annoying human they've ever spent time with in their lives?"

"No. Most people find me delightful." I plopped his ten-gallon hat on my own head and smiled prettily at him. To which I got an eye roll, naturally.

"Sorry, I don't do fanclubs."

"Your loss," I sing-songed. "Or we could make this interesting and play five-card stud if you aren't in the mood for talking. I've got a deck of cards in my purse."

He squinted at me. "You just carry around a deck of cards with you everywhere you go?"

I just stared back. "Yeah. Sometimes it takes a long time for food to come at restaurants. And some of us know how to have fun in our lives."

"While the rest of us are busy working."

"Oh, please," I said, reaching down between my feet and pulling up my purse. "I have a job that's starting after the wedding stuff slows down. A good job. Where I'll go into an office and everything."

"An office? Where you have to get dressed up and shit?"

"Yeah, where I get dressed up and shit. Some of us are actual grownups. We can't all just roll around in the mud with the cows our whole lives."

He guffawed. "That's rich coming from you. Plus, I can't think of anything more grown up than having the well-being of other living creatures resting on your shoulders. There's no days off, no down time, you know that. This new job, you get to kick off at what? Five o'clock every day?"

I sighed. This conversation was depressing me and that was the opposite of why I'd brought up my new job. I was trying to be excited about it. "I know. And I know I'm gonna miss being out with the animals and the rhythms of the ranch."

He frowned, not used to me backing down. "You couldn't find any other ranch work?"

I scoffed. "What am I gonna do, go try to be a hand somewhere? I'm used to running the joint. You know the pay's shit and where are they even gonna put me? In a bunkhouse? I don't think so." I shook my head. "I gotta go forward, and this is where it's taking me. I met the regional manager of this start up, FarmGro, when I interviewed. Rick's a great guy. He thinks I'll be a good fit."

"I bet he does," Jeremiah said under his breath.

I smacked him on the arm. "Not like that. Jesus."

He shrugged. "So what exactly are you gonna do for this Rick guy?"

"Nothing. I don't even work for him. I'll be a Precision Technology Specialist."

"A what now?"

"I'll do a bunch of things. Install software for growers, train them how to use it, and provide tech support. Then we'll collect all the data and maps and analyze everything. I'll do it all, start to finish, even traveling out to the farms to talk to them about what we've discovered about their yield cycles."

I was getting excited again talking about it. I'd actually be able to put my ag degree to use. Not at all in the way I *thought* I would by running my own ranch—but still in a really practical way that would help farmers get better usage out of their land, water, and resources. Rick had an amazing vision with his startup. He was basically trying to save the planet—in his small way, anyway. It was inspiring, and I was excited to be a part of it. Well, I was trying to be excited.

"So, what? You'll live in Austin and just drive out to farms in the hill country?"

I bit my lip as I shuffled the cards. "Well, I'll do my training in Dripping Springs shadowing with a Tech Specialist there, but if everything goes well, then I'll be moving to Fort Worth at the end of the year." Shit, why did I just tell him that? I looked up. "Don't tell Charlie, though. I haven't told her yet, what with the wedding and everything she's got on her plate right now."

Jeremiah's face was blank.

"At least you'll finally be rid of me, right?" I tried to joke.

"Don't you think your best friend deserves the truth? Especially since she sent the wedding gig your way. I thought the whole reason was so you could put down money for a house around here."

"I'm still gonna use the money for a down payment on a house. Just... not around here."

Jeremiah blew out a breath. "That's cold."

I blinked, cut by his judgement. "That's not fair. She's got her whole life ahead of her here. And I've got—" I threw my hands up in the air. "Nothing! Just memories. Not a future. Charlie would want the best for me. Sorry if that's too much for your pea brain to comprehend." I crossed my arms over my chest, the cards forgotten on the bench between us.

"Oh, my pea brain gets it well enough. I understand loyalty and family."

"Yeah, well," I cut my eyes toward his judgmental face, "all my family's dead."

He wasn't moved. "It's not just the people you're born to. Charlie's your family."

"It's not like I'm cutting her off. Why do you always have to be such an asshole? I'll come visit her every chance I get. People change and move apart. Just because you suffocate your brother and don't know how to let him have a life of his own doesn't mean that's how everybody does it."

I glared out my window, head turned away from him. If it wasn't pouring cats and dogs outside, I would've shoved out of the truck. Anything to get away from this asshole and his judgmental, asinine—

I waved a hand to fan myself. God, it was getting stuffy in here. I turned back toward Jeremiah, but only so I could reach across him and turn the key to the ignition.

"What are you doing?" he asked, sounding aggravated.

I glared at him. "Turning on the truck, duh. It's a thousand degrees in here and humid as hell. I need the A/C."

He put his hand on mine to stop me. "We don't have that much gas. You'll just have to suffer in silence, Princess."

To which I leaned over even further to look at his gas gauge. It was teetering at a little under a fourth of a tank. "Oh, that's rich," I said, withdrawing my hand. "So what was all that bullshit about never letting your tank get near a fourth because of the sediment, huh?"

He glared at me, his jaw tense. "If I hadn't been driving *your* ass around town all day long, I would've stopped to fill up."

"Yeah, right." I patted his thigh. "Or you love to be Mr. Know-It-All when really, you're just as human as the rest of us. Face it."

Again his hand came down toward mine, but instead of swatting it away, his big man paw clasped around my wrist. "Don't test me, little girl."

I could feel my pulse pounding underneath his grip.

I all but bared my teeth at him as I leaned into his space. "I'll test you if I want to. Maybe that's your problem. You don't have enough people in your life who dare talk back to you."

The space in the cab seemed to steam up even hotter, the windows all fogging as his eyes went dark. "I know one way to shut you up."

I smirked at him, feeling electricity race down my body. "I'd love to see you try."

And then he wrenched me forward into his lap and our lips smashed together.

4

Jeremiah

I was kissing Ruth. I hated Ruth. Ruth hated me.

But she was kissing me and tugging at the buttons on my worn denim shirt as if for once in our lives, we were on the exact same page.

And dammit, we were.

I grabbed her plump ass and dragged her all the way on top of me. The erection that had suddenly sprung up hard as iron was happy, so happy, to feel all of her soft, womanly heat against it.

Fuck, she felt good.

And these damn shorts she had on. I could reach right up them and there—oh fuck, there was her skin. Her ass. I squeezed it in my hands and gloried in how it felt. After all these goddamn months of watching her strut it in front of me.

Then she started sucking on my neck and *fuck*—

I yanked back from her and took her lips again cause if she kept sucking my neck like that, I was gonna embarrass myself and come before I meant to.

And now that this was finally fucking happening, no way was it gonna slip away from me.

After she had enough buttons undone on my shirt, I pulled it off over my head. It wasn't easy since it was still wet, and it near got stuck on my shoulders. But Ruth, for once in her life, was helpful instead of just laughing and nit-picking. She helped yank it off the rest of the way.

And then she pulled off her own and I had to stop, astounded by the perky fucking breasts that I'd only fantasized about heretofore.

I pressed her back to the steering wheel as I finally got my mouth on those tits. The horn honked and I didn't care, putting an arm around her back to brace her from the wheel as I licked and bit at her dusky pink nipple. The way she cried out and writhed on my lap told me she was liking everything I was doing.

She dug her hands into my hair and held me against her breast, so I suckled harder, and fuck, the way her nipple hardened into a tight peak under my tongue. She cried out in pleasure and that was it—I had to feel her.

The hand I had free I dove down to unbutton her shorts. She gyrated against my hand. It took way too fucking long to figure out the button, but I managed, and then I was slipping my hand down underneath her black lace panties.

I had to pull back and watch. She watched too as I slid my hand down her center. My work-tanned hand was dark against her pale belly. I'd exposed the top of her cunt and the sweet little curls there. Fuck, I loved a natural woman.

My breath caught as I slid my middle finger lower and I hit her moist center. She jerked forwards on my lap, her legs sliding open wider, her back arching.

"That's right, baby," I murmured, and when I glanced up, her eyes were wide and glazed.

I pulled my hand back from her center and sucked the finger drenched with her into my mouth. If I thought her eyes were lust-glazed before, it was nothing to when I did that. She jerked again on my lap and that was when I got it.

She'd never been fucked by a real man before, had she?

She was so intimidating; she'd probably only fucked little boys she thought she could control. Oh, honey.

I dropped my hand back down and I took my time, letting the anticipation build. And when I reached her center, I felt around for that little bud at the top of her slit.

Her entire body reacted when I made contact. Fuck, but she was so responsive. So on fire for it. For my touch.

How long since she'd properly shaken with a full-body orgasm? Maybe that was why she was wound so goddamn tight all the time.

I circled her clit lazily, massaging her lower back with my other hand, right at the top of her ass crack.

"W-why are we still wearing so many clothes?" she asked hoarsely.

"Because, sweetheart," I said, dipping my hand at her back lower so I was clutching one ass cheek and pulling her tighter to me. Simultaneously, as I felt more and more moisture slicking her center, I dipped my finger lower to massage around her entrance. "Some things are worth the fucking wait."

Her mouth dropped open like she was gonna say something else, but I shifted my hand in the front so I could really get deep and I slipped my finger inside her, feeling all along her fleshy walls as I went. And yep, there it was. The inside nubbin—the G spot. I started to massage around it while I dipped my head back to her breasts.

Rhythmically, I tugged her forward and backward over my pants-covered cock with my hand on her ass, other hand buried up her center. I surrounded her, owned her completely, and her responses rewarded me.

She became more and more lost to my caresses, to my command.

In the way I'd always fantasized she would.

Because I couldn't fucking lie anymore.

I'd dreamed about this. Far too many nights alone, knowing she was just down the hall. All the discipline it had taken not to open my door and walk the ten feet to her room seemed impossible now. How had I managed all those months not to make up some excuse so I could knock on her door? To see her in a robe she'd hastily pulled on, her cheeks flushed?

I'd dreamed of the way I'd peel that robe right off. Of how I'd shove her against the door, a hand over her mouth to make sure she didn't make a noise, just enough light to see the thrill and excitement in her eyes…

But it was too complicated. We'd lived in the same house. And then when she left and her best friend was marrying my brother—

I bit down hard on her nipple and she screamed. As she came. Hard.

I felt her contract deliciously around my hand.

I smiled and didn't let up. Because now here we were. Now here she was, her hot body over me. No, now that I finally had her in my arms, I wouldn't let up. Not until we'd both finally worked each other out of our damn systems.

Only when she was gasping and limp on top of me did I lift my head from her red, slightly abused nipples to look her in the eye.

"Do you want more?"

Her eyes were wide, pupils blown. She was still gasping for air. But she clenched her thighs around mine and obviously I hadn't done my job to the fullest because she was still clear-headed enough to be able to say, "Are you kidding? Fuck yeah, I want more. I'm on the pill and I'm clean. If you are too, then I want you to get out that big cock I can feel under my ass and fuck me with it."

5

Ruth

He still had his hand buried up my pussy and he never stopped circling as he looked me in the eye. "I'm not sure that's such a good idea, honey."

My body convulsed around his fingers at the word *honey*. I'd be mad about that later. Right now I just really needed him to fuck me. "Why not? I feel how hard you are."

"I'm not sure you can handle it the way I like it," he said. But he wasn't smirking or talking down to me. And his talented, oh-so-talented fingers were still teasing me.

The truth was, he'd just made me come harder than I ever had in my entire life. Even when I masturbated on my own. So he was nuts if he thought I was gonna let this go without pushing. "Whatever you can dish out, I can take."

One of his eyebrows just lifted. "There's not enough space in this cab."

I looked out the window. The rain wasn't letting up. I breathed out, difficult considering the way he was still playing with me. "Well, there's no one to see, is there. And I don't mind getting a little wet."

This time he did smirk, slipping his fingers back and forth inside me. "That's clear."

I breathed out hard. "So what are we waiting for?"

I wasn't sure exactly what I was asking for, but I knew in this moment I wanted it more than anything else I'd wanted in a long while. And when he shoved open his door, my heart rate spiked in thrilled excitement. Like I was about to go skydiving or bungee-jumping. God, that was what this felt like. Leaping into empty air, having no idea if I'd be caught on the other side.

But now that I'd given Jeremiah the go ahead, he was moving with sure movements. He rolled down the window, which I didn't understand at first. Until he unspooled the seatbelt and pulled it through the crack in the window.

We were far enough from the bridge and around a thickly forested curve that even if there were people stopped on the other side, we couldn't see them. More importantly, they couldn't see us.

And then Jeremiah's hands were on me, helping me down out of the truck and then yanking down my shorts and panties all at the same time. Rain drenched us both as he manhandled me. Still, I let him. Because I... I liked it.

And I liked watching him shuck his own jeans and boxers and toss them with my shorts back into the truck. He stood there, completely naked except for his boots, as rain pelted him. He had to be cold but his cock hung long and hard against his thigh. And he looked at me without shame, eyes dark and hooded as he skewered me with his gaze.

"Hands," he demanded.

Blinking, I held my hands forward. He gripped one wrist and jerked it up in a smooth but not rough motion. He reached back through the window for the seatbelt, pulling my hands above my head and looping the seatbelt around my wrists several times, pinning them above my head, my back to the truck.

And then he paused, grinning as the rain fell in sheets all around us, drenching us. He grabbed his cock and came toward me. Rain dripped down my face and ran into my open mouth.

In spite of the chill, I'd never been so hot. Being tied up in the middle of nowhere during a storm—it should have been crazy. And it was. Crazy fucking hot. Especially as this giant of a man came toward me with his huge cock and I knew exactly what he was going to do with it. Or thought I did.

Because yes, he came against me and lodged the tip of himself at my center. But he didn't immediately thrust inside. Instead, he grabbed my ass and hiked my leg up around him, pinning me between him and the truck.

"Finally," he growled through the noise of the pounding rain, "I have you exactly where I want you." He smacked at my breast from the underside and I jolted.

Whoa. This was exactly where he'd wanted me? For how long?

But there was barely a moment to form the question before he was continuing his barrage of my breasts. Soft smacks at first that turned more and more intentional.

His cock flexed at my center, the tip nudging inside just a little.

Still he didn't thrust, even as I moved restlessly against him with my hips. Good God, I'd never had anyone ever—well, do anything like any of this. I strained against the seatbelt pinning my wrists above my head. I wanted to touch him. To pull him to me, to scratch at his back. To do something to let out the wildness he was making rear up in me—a wildness I'd only glimpsed but never... never like this, and never with anyone else before.

When he reached down with both hands and grasped my buttocks finally lifting me—easily, I might add, and God but that was hot—against the truck, I arched my back toward him which pushed my breasts out.

"Is this what you want?" he asked, thrusting his hips forward just the tiniest bit so that I could feel more of him against my sex.

I nodded fervently as the rain continued pelting my face.

"Out loud," he demanded. Goddamn him.

"Just fuck me already," I shouted in his face.

He paused and smiled, a slow creeping smile, like he might just decide not to, now that he had me all trussed up and panting.

I narrowed my eyes at him, about to start swearing a blue streak, but then— "Oh!" I cried out as he finally thrust forward and filled me.

And when I say filled me, I do mean *filled me*. To the brim.

I was so full. Full of him.

He shoved deep to the root and it wasn't a kind of mindless fuck. Because while he held me pinned to the truck with one hand clutching my ass and his cock sheathed deep inside me, his other hand came to my face. He grasped me underneath my chin so that there was nothing to do except blink away the rain and look him dead in the eye as he began moving his hips, fucking me deep and hard.

Every slide of his shaft through my already incredibly sensitized pussy—oh God. And the way our chests slid together—the bristle of his chest hair against my nipples.

I arched toward him, trying to kiss him. Trying for anything to grasp back some of the control, but he just shook his head and gripped my chin tighter.

I got the message.

I wasn't in control here.

For our clashes outside of this moment, I could challenge him all I liked, but here, in this animal space of body against body, he was the alpha.

And I could submit and experience the most mind-blowing pleasure I'd never even known existed or—

I mean, there really was no other alternative. I wanted on this train for every stop, every inch of track laid until the bitter end.

But that still didn't mean I couldn't fucking tease him into getting what I wanted, though. So I stuck my tongue out and licked his thumb that was closest, toying with just the tip.

I felt his cock stiffen and jolt inside me. I was affecting him just as much as he was me. Good.

He let go of my chin, but only so he could grasp the hair at the nape of my neck and drag my head backward as he continued to fuck me, harder now, rougher.

And when his mouth dropped to the sensitive flesh of my neck, right above my collarbone—

I howled into the rain and came hard around his cock, clenching and milking him.

His head came up and, oh God, his face was glorious, all clenched and bulging veins as he threw his head back and grabbed my hips with both hands as he fucked me harder still, our hips slapping against one another until he emptied himself inside me.

He pulled out right away, and his cum slipped down the center of my legs.

He reached down between us and drew back up with his cupped hands, smearing the mixture of us all over my heaving breasts even as the rain immediately washed it away.

It was still the fucking hottest thing I'd ever seen in my life, and the mesmerized, satiated look on his face as he did it—holy shit!

An aftershock sent my legs spasming, and he looked up at me, a boyish grin on his face as he reached back down between my legs. Not for more cum this time but to massage me where I was so sensitive. I immediately cried out and shied back from him against the truck.

But he just shook his head at me. "You've got one more for me, I know you do."

My mouth dropped open and rain dribbled in over my lips, down my tongue. And he stood closer, his chest rubbing against mine as he worked two fingers inside me.

He was crazy. I'd already come twice, and so goddamn hard, I couldn't—

But then my entire body jolted as he started to massage that spot inside me. Jesus fuck, I'd thought the G-spot was an urban legend before tonight. And here he was, finding it time after time after—

I wailed as the orgasm started, my already sensitized body on edge and so ready for it.

And only now did he kiss me, swallowing and lapping up my lips and my tongue as I screamed, him never letting up those working, talented fingers of his.

It felt like minutes... or hours later after I'd collapsed on him, the world having gone so bright with the orgasm and then beautifully dim, rain dancing down my hot flesh, him cradling my head against his shoulder, that he finally traced his fingers up my arm and started unraveling the seat belt.

Oh... yeah. Right. I flexed my fingers, and they did feel a little numb. I blinked, feeling like I was coming back from a deep fog. What the—

He rubbed my hand to warm it up, and yeah, I guessed it was cold. I was actually cold all the way through really, standing out here in the rain. He released my other hand and I sort of fell against him. He was ready for me, though, and he caught me, one arm going underneath my shoulders and around my back.

"Here we go," he said gently, opening the door to the truck and helping me climb back in.

All my limbs felt limp as wet noodles. Seriously, what the hell? I'd never felt like this after sex. I mean, no, I'd never had toe-curling sex while being tied up in the middle of a rainstorm with Jeremiah Walker obviously, but still! What the fuck!

I crawled over to my side of the truck cab, glad now for the warmth inside.

Jeremiah came in after me. Our wet clothes were twisted on the floor of the cab. I shivered and crossed my arms over my chest, still blinking a little in shock at what we'd just done. I felt almost embarrassed to look at Jeremiah. We were both still completely buck naked.

"Come here," he said, breaking the silence, and I dared to look up at him. He had one arm held out.

When I didn't move, he slid over the bench seat toward me and pulled me into his arms. I collapsed against him.

He massaged my wrists and I jumped a little. They were sore, I hadn't even realized, from being bound in the seatbelts. I blinked up at him but he just pressed my head back down against his chest. "Hush now," he said, his voice deep and rumbling. "Just rest now."

And for once in my life, I didn't challenge him. I did what he said. I rested my head against his chest, listened to his steady heartbeat, and lost myself in the warmth of him.

6

Jeremiah

Holding her in my arms after what we'd just—

Fuck, I hadn't let myself go like that in... years. And she was the last woman in the world I ever expected to with, no matter my stupid fantasies.

I dropped my head back against the headrest.

This was a part of myself I'd pushed down successfully for so long. Why the hell did it have to bust out now? This goddamn woman. She'd pushed my buttons at every turn from the very beginning.

It was still no excuse. There was a reason I'd held myself back from pursuing anything with her. It was impossible.

But really, it was fine. We hadn't really done any damage. One wild fuck during a storm could be forgotten.

She'd wake up tomorrow morning and we'd put on our clothes and go back to hating each other. Everything would be normal again. We'd both forget this ever happened.

I could forget the warm grip of her body on my cock and the sweet way she'd given in to my every command. I *could*.

Or at least I could bury it down with all the other shit from my past that I never let see the light of day.

I'd be fine.

Everything would be *fine*. Just like always. Just like I always made it.

I closed my eyes and tried to drift. It was uncomfortable and cramped in the cab but at least outside the rain had finally slowed. Still hadn't stopped, but it had slowed as the sun set and full dark settled all around us.

I should've made her drink some water before I let her fall asleep. I'd make sure she did when she woke up.

My cock was thick and hard underneath her—I wasn't sure how it was supposed to be anything else with a hot, gorgeous woman sprawled across me.

But eventually I was able to drift off. I didn't know how long for when suddenly Ruth was stirring on top of me and sitting up.

And then freaking out.

"Holy shit. Holy shit, holy shit, holy shit," she just kept saying over and over. She tumbled off of me.

"What?" I asked. She just kept saying, "holy shit," though, and before I could stop her, she'd opened her car door and was scrambling out.

"Ruth, Jesus, where the fuck do you think you're going?"

"I've gotta pee," she shouted back at me.

"Do you even know where you're going? Take your phone at least for a light!"

"I'm fine!"

I huffed out a frustrated breath, then followed her anyway. She could get over me seeing her piss. I wasn't letting her out of my sight. We were basically in the middle of the woods, and this was bobcat country. I'd seen one out on the ranch a couple months back. She'd lived here all her life so she knew it too.

There was barely a sliver of moonlight out so I was only moving by the sound of her footsteps and the rustle of bushes near the edge of the road.

"I won't look," I said.

She shrieked, jumping up. "Jesus, I told you to stay in the truck!"

"Actually, you said you were fine, and I determined you'd be safer if I came along. The buddy system is best in the wilderness."

She scoffed. "I'm barely fifteen feet from the truck!"

"And I feel better when I'm close."

"Jesus, you really are a control freak."

I didn't bother denying it.

"Hold your hands over your ears. I don't want you listening to me pee."

I rolled my eyes, not that she could see it. "I'm a guy. I've heard plenty of people pee before."

"Not me!"

"Fine." Anything to get her back in the truck. I put my hands over my ears. I could just make out her crouching back down.

I dutifully waited until she stood back up. "My turn."

She made a disgusted noise. "I'm sure you'll be fine against the woodland creatures. I'll be in the truck."

"Get some water from the back. I don't want you getting dehydrated."

"Control freak," she hissed under her breath as she passed. I could just make out her shaking her head. I could also make out her breasts jiggling. I quickly looked away. Having a hard-on wouldn't help me at the moment.

But right then, a wolf howled, I couldn't tell how near. And she grasped for my bicep. "How about you bring the water in. I'll be in the truck cab." And then I heard her scrambling steps as she raced back to the truck.

After she was gone, all I could feel was the heat of her touch ghosting against my arm. She'd been afraid and she'd reached for me. It was disturbing how much I liked that. I quickly took care of business and then climbed up into the back of the truck to retrieve the two now-full bottles of water.

Ruth was huddled in the corner of her side of the cab when I climbed back in. She was holding up her shirt and shaking it out.

"Still wet?" I asked, knowing it was.

"Do you think it'll be dry by morning?"

"We could turn on the truck for a while and put the shirts over the vents. The denim probably won't be dry till morning. Maybe not even then."

"Even just getting my bra and underwear dry would be a start," she said. "And having some light for a little bit. It's so dark and creepy out here." We were close enough that I could feel her shudder. It made me want to pull her back in my arms but then I reminded myself that, right, that was over and done with. That was how it had to be.

I reached for the keys and started up the ignition. "Watch your eyes, gonna turn on the light."

I punched on the overhead light. When I looked over at Ruth, goddamn, I was smacked all over again by the beauty of her, acres of beautiful pale skin. The way she was curled up, I couldn't see much except her long legs and the side of her ass. I immediately glanced away, though pulling my eyes off her took effort.

"Here, I'll turn on the heat," I said, keeping my eyes averted. "You can put your, uh, underthings against the vents to get them dry."

"'Kay. Thanks."

I felt her scramble beside me and it had never been so difficult to be a gentleman.

Finally she was holding up the thin scraps of the little lacy thing she called a bra and her cotton panties against the two vents on her side.

"Wanna hand me your shirt? I can hold it up to these vents. And here, some water." I handed her one of the full bottles of water we'd collected earlier.

"Oh. Sure. Thanks."

How had we gone from bickering to wild sex to this stilted politeness? All I could say was that I hoped she was also doing the genteel thing and not looking 'cause my cock had a mind all its own and cared fuck-all about being gentlemanly. All it knew was that the slick cunny he'd been buried in hours ago was feet away and he wanted to be buried back there. Especially as I watched her throat as she swallowed. I reached blindly for the other bottle and drank some too.

It was from a distraction. Not when I was locked in this space with her. In spite of all my good intentions, I was hard. I tried to adjust myself but I wasn't small, and yeah, buck naked here.

Out of my peripheral vision, I could tell that Ruth was handing me her shirt, so I reached out for it.

And as our fingers made contact, she gasped.

I didn't think about it, it was instinctual. I looked over at her face to make sure she was okay. Which was when I saw where she was looking—straight at my lap. My cock jumped at seeing the way her mouth had dropped open, at the glimpse of her sweet little pink tongue.

Then she yanked her eyes up to mine and she realized she'd been caught. Her chest heaved up and down.

And my control snapped.

Fuck restraint.

"Touch yourself," I growled.

"What?" she gasped.

"I wanna see how you touch yourself when you're alone. Do it."

Her breath hitched. And then she dropped the items she was holding to the vents and her hand moved haltingly down her body.

"What are we doing?" she whispered.

"You're touching your pussy and showing me how you make yourself come. That's what we're doing. And then I'll probably fuck you again," I answered honestly.

Her body spasmed at my words and her legs fell open, exposing fully in the light of the cab what I'd only been able to glimpse earlier.

And Jesus *fuck,* but she had a beautiful pussy.

"That's right," I said low and dark. "Spread yourself and show me."

She let out a little moan but did what I said.

"Fuck," I whispered, glad I'd just drunk some water because already my mouth felt dry.

Her pussy was beautiful, petal pink, and so wet she glistened in the light. The juxtaposition of her—acerbic Ruth, always ready to bite my head off—with her face all soft and vulnerable, opening her legs wide to me.

I swallowed hard and clenched my fist so I didn't reach out for her. Not yet. No, I'd have my show first.

"Touch yourself," I said again, my voice raw and brusque. "Make yourself come. I wanna see."

I knew the moment her middle finger made contact with her flesh, because her entire body jolted.

My gaze flew up from her hand to her face, where her hazel eyes were smoky as they watched me watching her. But immediately they dropped and a blush rose to her cheeks. I'd embarrassed her.

But she didn't stop touching herself. She was no wilting flower. She was Ruth. Bold, ballsy, take no prisoners. Even now. Because she was daring to do this, to do the one thing I knew terrified her most—submit to me.

And so I watched, eyes glued to her as she closed her eyes and bit the nubbin in the center of her top lip. She didn't try to be like a porn star. At first, she barely made a sound. And she didn't grab at her breasts or run her hands up and down her body.

Not until the end, anyway, when the hand not grinding at her clit rose to her breast. She didn't palm it gently or plump it in a way I'd seen women do before. No, it was clear she was doing what I'd asked.

She squeezed the tips of her breasts *hard*, then harder still, forcing her nipples into stiff peaks, plucking at the other breast when it didn't harden as quickly as she wanted. She started writhing on the seat, squeezed her nipple and worked her pussy—and then came the cries.

"Oh— oh God. *Fuck—*"

Her eyes flew open, like she was surprised at how hard the orgasm was hitting her. And when they did, her eyes made searing contact with mine.

Enough was enough. I was hard as a goddamned stone, and seeing that she could just allow herself to come apart so genuinely like that in front of me, without artifice or pretending—goddammit, this *woman*—

I shifted on the seat, one hand on my cock, and I guided my seeking tip toward her dripping center.

Her eyes went wide again as I came near. It wasn't fear I saw there, but again that surprise. Maybe it was still the surprise that kept sparking through me. Was this really happening. Ruth— Me and—

Ruth's bared breasts and legs wide to receive—

My stiff cock brushing against the wet lips of her vulva.

Her eyes rolled at the contact and she moaned, reaching a hand to guide me toward her. I gave my head a shake and reached, grasping her around the wrist.

No touching, I said by pressing her wrist back against the seat back.

Her eyes flared and I smiled, snatching her other wrist up. She sucked in a breath and for a moment, her bicep flexed against my grip, like she might pull away. But in the end, it was only a moment of tension, her dark eyes flashing to mine before she gave in to me.

The power that swelled in my chest from her giving in, especially knowing it was a sacrifice willingly given—oh, I would reward her.

"Tell me you want it," I demanded. "Beg."

"P-please," she said, her voice shaking a little. "Please fuck me."

I braced my knee on the bench seat, shifted her underneath me, and slid home.

7

Ruth

BY THE TIME the sun rose, I was aching, sore, and had come more times in a twelve-hour period than I ever imagined was possible.

It was... uh, definitely one way to pass the time while being stranded between two suddenly roaring rivers.

We'd barely slept—just brief naps against Jeremiah's chest before either he or I would reach for one another again. And then we'd rearrange ourselves in the small cab. Me on my back on the bench seat. Me riding him while he sat in the passenger's seat, hands clenching my thighs. Me on my hands and knees while he stood on the nerf bar step up into the truck, driving so deep his balls slapped my ass.

I had been thoroughly fucked, eaten out, massaged, and then... cuddled.

Cuddled by Jeremiah.

We'd obviously entered into some strange pocket universe outside of normal time and space. That was all I could think as I looked, exhausted, out the window as the sun rose, pink streaking the finally clear sky.

Jeremiah stirred underneath me. I was sleeping all but on top of him, though I was shocked he'd been comfortable enough to actually fall asleep, lounged half on the bench, his long legs bent awkwardly into the footwell below—and with me tucked behind and half on top of him.

I scooted back against the door to give him space to sit up.

We were still both absolutely naked.

He blinked and rubbed a fist against one eye. "Morning already? We should check the stream to see if it's passable."

Right. The stream. It was such a shockingly prosaic proposition that it took me a second to answer.

"Wanna hand me my shirt?" he asked.

Of course. He couldn't exactly walk over to check the stream naked. What if a car was stopped on the other side, waiting for the water to lower?

Because shit, it was officially tomorrow.

And that meant it was time to go back to the real world.

I was just handing Jeremiah his shirt and pulling mine back on over my head after securing my bra when—

A truck drove past.

My head swung to Jeremiah, eyes wide.

"I guess the water's lowered enough that it's passable," Jeremiah said.

"No shit." Still, I blinked a couple times as Jeremiah reached down into the passenger wheel well for his boxers and jeans.

I scrambled for my underwear and shorts. The underwear were more dry than the denim shorts but I pulled them both on anyway.

Jeremiah had to step out of the truck to put his jeans back on and I averted my gaze from his taut bare ass as he climbed out, my cheeks flaming.

Which was ridiculous, considering what we'd been doing all evening. I mean, we'd used some napkins he had stashed in his glove compartment to clean me up, but I was still messy with his cum, he'd emptied into me so many times. My breath caught at the memories and I was torn between wanting to run to a shower right away and wanting to linger with the scent of him all over me for the day at least as a reminder to prove to myself that this had all actually *happened.*

If not for the soreness between my legs, I might be tempted to think it was all a fever dream.

Especially when Jeremiah climbed back in the truck, his face completely composed and no-nonsense.

"We should hurry back to the ranch. They'll be worried about us not coming home last night."

I nodded, reaching down and pulling my cell phone out. "I'll call them as soon as we— Well, I would have if my battery hadn't died."

Jeremiah reached for his phone and plugged it into a wire coming from the center console as he turned on the truck. "You can text them from my phone as soon as we get somewhere there's service."

I nodded, looking at my lap.

Then he'd pulled the truck into drive and we were pulling forward, the trailer behind us clanking as it tugged along.

We rounded the corner and there was the stream that had trapped us last night. White water raced underneath the bridge, but at least it was an inch below the road now. It must have only just become passable.

Jeremiah took it slow as our truck and trailer rattled over, and then, just like that, we were on the other side. I couldn't help looking over my shoulder out the back window.

It didn't look like anything special, so why did I feel like our night back there had changed everything? I snuck a look at Jeremiah, but his face was unreadable.

I was just opening my mouth to ask what all this meant, if we were supposed to pretend like last night hadn't happened or what, when Jeremiah reached over and switched the radio on to a morning news station.

They talked about the night rainstorms that had caused flash-flooding in the area.

He didn't say anything else. He'd been so kind and accommodating last night, why couldn't he sense I needed him to say something about all that had happened?

I started to reach out for him, maybe to touch his arm or his thigh. He must have sensed me because his head whipped my direction. "Don't touch me," he snapped.

I jerked my hand back. *Okay.* So he was still a jackass outside of... outside of the things we'd done last night. I turned my head away from him, glaring out my passenger's seat window, not wanting to let on how much that hurt.

Had my body literally just been a way for him to amuse himself when he was bored? Then I shook my head. Fuck not getting answers. A man couldn't— He couldn't just dominate me like that and then—

"So what the hell was that last night?" I asked, my voice coming out more combative than I intended.

His gaze didn't veer away from the road as he drove slowly, carefully, on the still rain-slicked roads. While the drizzle had slowed through the night, it must have only stopped for good maybe an hour ago.

Finally, his heavy eyes came my direction. "Last night can be whatever you want it to be," he finally said as his eyes moved back to the road as we rounded a particularly sharp curve.

I crossed my arms over my chest. "And what the hell is that supposed to mean?"

"Well," he said, tilting his head. "It's clear there's some"—he shook his head like he didn't know how to finish the thought—"some chemistry between us. We can choose to explore that. Be friends with benefits, as it were. Or we can forget last night ever happened. It's up to you."

I snorted, propping one knee up on the dash. "Oh, sure. Let's just forget you came in me so many times last night not even the napkins could keep up by the end. Frankly, I didn't know that was possible for men. Four times in one night?" I shook my head, my belly tightening. "Shit."

That had his head whipping toward me *real* fast. And the way his jaw was tight as his eyes quickly tracked up my thigh before his head jerked back to look out the front windshield told me he wouldn't be forgetting any time soon, either.

"I'm not my brother," he stated gruffly, eyes still firmly on the road. "I don't do hearts and flowers. Or engagement rings."

That had me cracking up. I literally slapped my knee I was laughing so hard. "Slow down, cowboy. And I always wondered why you never had any dates. Mystery solved."

I shook my head, my giggles slowing. "As far as I understood, we were just talking about scratching each other's itches. Stress relief." I yawned and stretched. Because God, I hadn't realized what a bundle of stress I'd been, what with all the wedding prep and trying to find a job for the last six months. The part-time job I'd taken as a barista to pay my half of the rent didn't count.

But all my limbs felt completely relaxed. Okay, I was a little sore from using muscles I hadn't for a while, but it was a good sore. And I felt like I could sleep for twenty-four hours. Easy sleep, though, not the restless tossing and turning I'd been doing lately.

"Stress relief," he repeated, considering, and then he nodded as if he liked the sound of it.

He shot a quick glance my way. "Is this us actually agreeing on something for once?"

I smirked at him. "Don't get used to it, buddy. I only submit in the bedroom. Or the truck cab, as it were."

"Or wherever else I manage to corner you alone," he murmured under his breath.

And my own breath caught.

I smiled secretly to myself. Well, well, well. I'd been dreading the next couple weeks if I was honest with myself. I mean, I wanted to see my friend get married, of course I did. But managing it all was intimidating, though of course the money would be a godsend.

But now... now, I felt a prickle of anticipation for what was to come.

8

Ruth

Several days later, Charlie and I stood in Austin Bergstrom Airport waiting for her to pick up her parents.

Charlie checked her phone again. "Any minute now." She bit her bottom lip anxiously as she looked up the escalator at the arrivals streaming down.

We'd been working on getting their suite ready back at the house almost nonstop. So nonstop that Jeremiah and I hadn't had any time to sneak away to explore... well, whatever it was we'd started during our spontaneous overnight.

Everyone had been worried about us when we got back the next day, but more than that, they'd been surprised when we told them what happened that we'd actually managed to spend almost 24 hours together without choking each other.

I'd mostly managed not to blush and bit my tongue against commenting that I'd choked on Jeremiah's cock when I'd briefly deep throated him, but it had been quite mutually pleasant.

Outwardly, we'd gone on bickering like usual, but the occasional hot looks he'd shoot me would make my toes squirm in my sneakers—and give me a shot of adrenaline to keep on keeping on.

The four of us—me, Charlie, Reece, and Jeremiah—had been up till past two a.m. last night finishing up the last touches on the parents-in-law suite. Charlie and I were decorating while the boys finished up the plumbing work in the attached bath.

By the end of the night the room looked like something out of a magazine. And the toilet flushed! So it was a win all around.

"Don't worry so much, it's gonna go great." I reached down and squeezed Charlie's hand.

She looked over at me. "You think? I haven't seen them since May and that was only for a few hours when Reece and I stopped by on our vacation in San Francisco. I'm not really sure my mother and I can stand being in each other's presence for much longer than that."

"You don't have to be," I assured her quickly. "I'm here to be your shield. Anytime you need. The wedding's in five days anyway. And then you're off on your honeymoon."

"Still." Her eyes went wide. "Five *days*."

I grinned at her. "And then you'll be married to your man."

Her face eased into a smile and her shoulders relaxed. "That part I can't wait for. Everything this year's been such a whirlwind. I mean, eight months ago, I didn't even know him. But now I can't imagine life without him."

"Which is hilarious because it took you two forever to get together."

"But once we did," she laughed, "there was no going back. He's my one." She got that starry-eyed look in her eyes she always did whenever she talked about Reece. "As soon as I got out of my own way, I could see that."

But then she looked back up at the escalator full of people and started nervously nibbling on her lip again. "If only I can get to the happily-ever-after part."

"Girl! Don't worry. It's only five days! I've got a ton planned, plus there will be more and more people coming in to help take the heat off you ever having too much one-on-one time with your mom. The guys' boss and his family will be coming in tomorrow, and they're bound to be a great distraction."

She nodded rapidly. "Yeah. Yeah. You're right. There's nothing to worry about." I wasn't sure who she was trying to convince, me or herself.

"Besides, my car's still in the shop, so there's always the excuse of needing you to drive me around to check on catering or something. If she ever starts driving you crazy, just give me a hand motion, and I'll say I need you to drive me somewhere."

Charlie's forehead scrunched up. "But you don't need me to drive you. You know you can borrow my car anytime. I borrowed yours often enough before I got mine."

I lifted an eyebrow significantly. "Mom doesn't know that."

Charlie laughed. "When do you get your car back, anyway?"

I made a face. "I don't know. They called and said something had gummed up the engine, they weren't sure what. But God, don't tell Jeremiah. He'll just get all holier than thou about how I shouldn't have always run my car barely above empty and let the sediment or whatever pile up on the bottom of the gas tank."

Charlie rolled her eyes. "You two will have to put aside your differences and make friends *sometime*. You're my maid of honor and he's Reece's best man, for God's sake! You'll be walking down the aisle on his arm."

A little shiver went down my spine at the thought, but I shook the feeling away, quickly reassuring her. "Don't worry, we'll behave ourselves."

"You better."

"You worry too much."

She shrugged, her eyes narrowing. "Shit," she said under her breath. "There they are."

She pasted on a big plastic-looking smile and lifted her hand to wave. I followed her gaze to the top of the escalator where an impeccably dressed woman in a cream-colored pantsuit stood stiffly beside a harried-looking man clutching onto several large pieces of luggage.

Her mother strode off the escalator once it reached the bottom while her husband struggled to get the luggage off, creating a small bottleneck until he was able to shove the two large suitcases forward while dragging another behind him, along with another carryon and a large duffel on top of them.

Charlie had jumped forward, but her dad was free by then, and suddenly there was her mom, right in front of us.

"Darling," her mother said, and then her eyes scanned Charlie head to toe, her mouth tightening into a line of obvious disapproval. "You look... well."

"Hi Mom," Charlie responded, her voice sounding odd, at least to me. "Dad," she said with more warmth as she maneuvered around the tall statue that was her mother. "Here, let me help you with those."

"Oh, that's not necessary—"

But Charlie had already unburdened him of two of the largest suitcases. I rushed forward to take one from her.

They stood in front of each other a little awkwardly until Charlie finally went in for a hug. She hugged her dad first, then, both of them stiff, her mother.

"This is my best friend, Ruth. She's the wedding planner I told you about."

I gave a little wave.

Her mother's scrutinizing eyes came my way, and like she had with her daughter, she gave me the once over. She didn't bother hiding the fact that she found what she saw lacking.

Then again, with the perfect make-up and hair she had going on, it probably wasn't surprising that she wasn't into my t-shirt, jeans, and boots.

Still. She could've been a little less obvious about it. Charlie had tried to warn me about her mom, but I didn't think she'd actually be such a caricature in real life. But apparently Napa Valley Rich Bitch had been the perfect moniker after all.

I smiled brightly, determined to make the time with this lady stress-free for Charlie. "This way. We aren't parked far."

Charlie's mom exchanged a long-suffering look with her father. "I told you we could call a car."

And I caught Charlie's exasperated glance. Picking her mom up from the airport was supposed to be a nice thing, but this lady was a real trip.

"Nonsense," I said, still smiling over-brightly. "Plus, it'd be too easy for a car service to get lost in the hill country when GPS cuts in and out. And this way you and Charlie can get started catching up. It's going to be a busy week. We've got all sorts of things on the itinerary."

"Oh," her mother said, looking slightly mollified as she pulled out her phone. "I didn't receive an itinerary."

Aha. Right. "Well," I said, tugging the heavy suitcase along behind me as I led the way out of the airport. "I'm still solidifying the details on some activities, but then I'll shoot it right over to you. What's your email?"

I'd shoot that email right as soon as I, ya know, actually wrote down the itinerary and made it all nice and pretty looking, considering at the moment the planned activities were just jotted down on a bunch of sticky notes all over my and Charlie's apartment.

"Why tell you now when you have nowhere to write it down?" her mother asked coldly. "Really, I would have thought you'd have covered this detail by now. How is everyone supposed to coordinate their schedules when we have no idea what to expect one moment to the next?"

Well, considering you're basically on vacation, lady, I didn't think you'd have much of a schedule to coordinate, but I just smiled and nodded. "Great point. I'll get right on it."

Things just got better and better once we got out to the parking lot and to Charlie's car.

She'd been so proud of being able to save up enough money to buy it a couple months ago—a fifteen-year-old Honda Civic with some hail damage and a hundred thousand miles on it that she'd named Rhonda. She kept it pristinely clean inside and couldn't have been prouder if it were her own child. Considering where she'd been only six months earlier, homeless and on the run, I supposed it made sense.

And the way her mother stopped and looked clearly appalled at the car made me officially hate the lady.

"I know it's not much," Charlie said quickly, rushing forward to unlock the passenger seat and open the door for her mother. "But I was able to save up my own money and not go into any debt for it. I know you always say that's important, especially since I was getting a new start here. And I actually got a really good deal. There was a little bit of cosmetic damage from hail on the roof so I got it for a steal—"

Her mother made a scoffing noise. "It's hard to steal something they were no doubt trying to *give* away."

I saw the hurt register on Charlie's face before she laughed like her mom had told a joke. My hand clenched around the luggage handle I was holding. Her mother made a noise of distaste. "Well, I hope it's clean at least," she said before sweeping herself into the front seat.

Charlie didn't meet my eye as she popped the trunk and headed there to put the luggage inside. I joined her, leaning over close so her dad couldn't hear. "You okay?"

She flashed a smile that didn't meet her eyes. "Fine." She hefted the heavy suitcase and I helped her lodge it in the trunk.

"Here, Dad, I got that," she said, reaching for the suitcase he still stood holding awkwardly to the side of the car. He handed it over passively. I got the feeling that was his role in the family. Standing by silently.

I helped Charlie get all the bags into the car and then joined her dad in the backseat for the World's Most Awkward Half Hour Drive to get back to the ranch.

Charlie tried pointing out landmarks along the way.

Her mother was supremely uninterested and spent most of the time on her phone.

Bitch Status confirmed. I swear, if this woman wasn't paying for the wedding, I'd be severely tempted to give her a piece of my mind.

I'd never been big on tact. I'd have to be on my best behavior for the next week.

Her dad just sat like a lump beside me looking out the window. Did the guy even have a personality? Or maybe he had once, but it had just been shaved down over time by being forced to be a lapdog to his wife. Weird freaking dynamics. No wonder Charlie had wanted out of her childhood home as quick as she could. Unfortunately, she'd landed in the clutches of a monster, only recently escaping.

She deserved all the good things coming to her, and I determined all over again to make this week as smooth as possible for her, mother-of-the-bride-from-hell or not.

I could all but feel Charlie's relief when we pulled up to the ranch gate. "I'll get it," I said, jumping out to unlatch it.

I hauled the gate open and waited for the car to drive through, closing and locking it behind them before hopping back in. Just in time to hear her mother commenting, "I'm just saying, a manual gate? What century are we living in?"

"Things are different out here, Mom," Charlie said, and I could hear the tension in her voice. "There's no need to waste money on things that aren't important."

"What if it's raining?" her mother asked. "You still have to get out in the mud to haul open the gate? What if you're in heels?"

Charlie didn't answer, because obviously, yes, we did. And heels weren't usually ranch attire.

"That's the good thing about Texas," I piped up. "Most of the year not much rain."

"Except for when it rains so much there are *tornados*," her mother answered acerbically.

I barely bit back the retort that the tornado in question had done the world a favor by getting rid of her asshole former son-in-law, but that probably wouldn't win me any brownie points.

"Just a few more minutes now," I said brightly as the car bumped up the long gravel road. "I think you'll really like the suite we've prepared for you."

A noise came from Mrs. Winston's throat as if she'd believe it when she saw it.

I turned my head toward the window so no one would see me roll my eyes.

Minutes later, we were finally pulling up in front of the house. From the outside, you couldn't tell it was only half complete inside. It was two stories, like the original, but unlike the original, it didn't have a wraparound porch yet, or much in the way of landscaping.

We'd all been working so hard to get the inside finishing touches done, I hadn't really stepped back to think about what a first impression of the place might make...

But now as we drove up, I had to admit... It wasn't as impressive as one might hope. Not nearly what it would be once it was all finished up. It just sort of looked like a big square box with some windows cut out. The siding had been painted blue, but there hadn't been any shutters or window treatments put on yet.

"It's really nice inside," Charlie said defensively, obviously doing exactly what I was—looking at the house through her mother's eyes. Which was bullshit, because before now, we'd all been proud of the progress being made. Especially with the blood, sweat, and tears we'd all been putting into it lately.

"I see," her mother said, that note of distaste again in her voice.

I shoved out of my car door, casting my eyes again to the sky. *Lord help me not to strangle this woman. Give me patience.*

Reece came out the front door of the house, obviously having heard the sound of the engine. He waved at everyone in the car, a big, genuine Reece smile on his face.

He was in jeans and a white undershirt that were covered in drywall dust. He went over to stand by Charlie once everyone had gotten out of the car and congregated near the hood. He put an arm around Charlie and flashed his white-toothed grin at her parents.

"Mrs. Winston. Mr. Winston. Good to see you again. Welcome to the ranch."

Mrs. Winston gave him her characteristic once over and didn't seem pleased, but then, I wasn't sure pleased was an expression her facial features could actually make.

"Surely, we aren't such a surprise that you couldn't finish getting dressed, young man."

Reece gave a guffaw. "You're funny, Mrs. Winston." He shook his head as if she'd actually been making a joke—either that or he was just really good at diffusing tension. "I was just working on installing some drywall upstairs. Come on in, we've got your rooms all ready."

He pulled back from Charlie and waved them inside. But when Charlie started toward the trunk, he said, "You take your parents inside, babe. I got the bags."

The little smile of thanks she passed him before turning back toward her parents was a small thing—but it still hit me in the gut. There were a million little communications like that that passed between partners, real partners, that I wondered if I'd ever have.

"Well, I think you guys have it from here," I said. "I'll check back in for the last dress fitting tomorrow." I looked Charlie's way. "Let me know if you need anything. My phone's always on."

She nodded significantly. She was staying on here at the ranch in another of the rooms we'd just managed to finish renovating—well, we'd at least gotten a mattress in there—but she'd still be sharing a bathroom with her parents.

Tomorrow was a big day. Not only was there the dress fitting, but the twin's boss, Xavier, and his family, came into town. They were traveling in an RV so we didn't have to find accommodations for them, just a hook up to water, which we had.

Speaking of... I needed to go double check the site was all ready, and that we had extra provisions, and that the stables were ready, because they were bringing horses—

I needed to find Jeremiah.

Behind me, Charlie's mother was fussing about her shoes getting muddy on the walk up to the house and I felt glad to be walking away from that disaster, and then guilty about leaving Charlie alone with it. Then again, 'it' was her mother, not mine. Besides, she had Reece there as a buffer now.

And if this wedding was going to get pulled off, I couldn't mother-sit twenty-four-seven.

I ducked into the barn, but there was only Buck, doing something with some rope. "Hey, you seen Jeremiah around?"

He looked up startled, his eyes widening when he saw it was me. "What?"

"Jeremiah? You know where he is?"

He just kept staring at me. I tapped my foot impatiently. "Any day now."

"Stables," he finally mumbled. "Think I saw him in the stables."

I turned with a wave of thanks and headed out across the small, weedy dirt path back toward the stables.

And yep, there was Jeremiah. It was nearing the end of a blazing hot Texas day and he'd taken his shirt off as he worked inside the stables. The doors were open on either end and he had a fan on, so there was a breeze. But it was apparently doing little to cool the sweat dripping down the canyon between his muscled shoulders.

I cleared my throat and he turned around from where he'd been spreading fresh hay out in a stall.

The sight of him was even more glorious from the front. Strong, hugely wide chest. Narrowing down to his slim waist and tight, sculpted abs.

I'd just cleared my throat, but it still felt too dry.

And I realized I was standing here looking him up and down, just like Mrs. Winston had me. But I imagined the look on my face was far from distaste.

When I finally lifted my eyes back to Jeremiah's, he wasn't looking at me like he felt distaste either. No, his eyes were blazing.

"Wanna scratch an itch?" I asked.

He threw down the pitchfork he'd been stabbing into the straw and strode toward me. "Thought you'd never ask."

Before I barely knew what was happening, he had me up against the wall of the stable, all his hard, hot, damp flesh pressing into me.

"Fuck, you're hot when you dress like this." He massaged my ass through my jeans.

I laughed and looked down at myself. I was wearing a completely non-descript blue t-shirt, jeans, and boots. "Like a ranch hand?"

"Like the sexiest fucking ranch hand I ever saw," he said, before his mouth came down on mine.

I opened to him and the stress of the day fell away. Monster mothers of the bride, all the shit I still had to coordinate, all the emails waiting to be sent—*poof*. Gone in a wisp of smoke as I opened my legs to Jeremiah and he took every inch I gave.

He slid in between my legs and his hands dropped down between us, first working at my button and then his own. His fingers being anywhere near my sex had me tingling.

But it wasn't until he pulled me away from the wall and manhandled me so that I was bent over a nearby sawhorse that my blood really got pumping.

He leaned over my back and whispered in my ear, breath hot against the wisps of hair escaping my ponytail, "You'll want to hold on. I don't know that I can take it easy on you. Your safeword is *red*. Tell me your safeword."

"Red," I gasped out, my eyes wide as saucers. I was glad I was faced away from him. I didn't want him to see the excited shock on my face at the way he was— I'd never had any man be like this with me. And I'd had no clue that I'd respond like this. I was immediately wet. Drenched, in fact.

"Now don't say it again unless you mean it," he said, his voice low and growly.

I nodded.

"Out loud."

"Yes. I mean I won't. Not unless I mean it."

"Good girl," he growled, and the tone of his voice echoed throughout my body, like I could feel the vibrations of it in my sex.

I wiggled my ass against him and he laughed, low.

"Always pushing the boundaries, aren't you, little brat?"

I looked over my shoulder at him. "Maybe I just want to get fucked and you're stalling."

He'd lifted back to standing and he kicked my feet to open wider as I stayed sprawled over the sawhorse. I had to grab onto the wooden legs for balance and that made him smile. I barely just bit back a curse, and that was because I saw him slowly, ever so slowly sliding his belt out of its straps.

"W-what are you going to do with that?" I asked. I couldn't tell if I was scared or excited. I was suddenly feeling a thousand things at once. One thing was for damn sure—I felt alive. More alive than I'd felt in... well, a long time. I bit my bottom lip against the anticipation.

"Good girls wait and see. Bad girls are impatient."

He dragged down my jeans in one motion, panties with them, exposing my bare bottom.

"Well, isn't that a pretty little ass. But I can make it prettier."

And he smacked me with his bare palm, upward from underneath my right ass cheek, so that it wobbled and jiggled obscenely. And then he did the same to the other cheek.

Oh my God. I felt mortified. I had never had my bits *jiggled* so remorselessly. Even more appalling?

How motherfucking *amazing* it felt.

I wanted him to do it again. And again.

I'd always thought of ass slapping as degrading. I didn't realize it could actually feel... so damn erogenous.

But Jeremiah, damn him, he missed nothing. "You liked that, didn't you?"

I kept my face down, hidden, trying to keep some of my dignity, but he just leaned over my back so he had access to my face. He nipped at my ear, then my jaw. "Tell the truth," he breathed.

I squeezed my eyes shut but admitted, "Yes. Please. It felt so good."

"Good girl."

He pulled back and then smacked me again, the same way. It smarted a little more since the flesh was sensitive, but he was on a roll now. He kept smacking me—spanking me.

Oh my God, he was *spanking me*.

And all I could do was bend over further and wiggle my ass toward him, begging for more of his touch.

Especially when in between spanking me, he'd caress my ass and reach a hand down in between my legs, teasing his strong fingers along the rim of my slick sex. He'd tease, tease, tease a little more, a little closer to where I needed him...

And then he'd pull back and wallop me again.

Until I was whining with the need to come. And eventually begging.

"Please, Jer, please fuck me. Come on, you're torturing me. I just need to come. Please just let me come." I twisted on my feet as his fingertips ran up and down my no-doubt pink ass.

"You think you deserve my cock now?"

"Yes," I said. "I deserve it. *You* deserve it."

He huffed out a laugh. "That's certainly fucking true." He breathed out heavily. "But first you learn who's in charge here. And that's me. You, on the other hand, still need to learn who's your Master. So will you take the bit?"

"The bi—?" I started, but then he held up his belt, loosely looped. As I watched on, he dipped it over my head and then, when I didn't struggle or say no, he demanded, "*Open*." I opened my mouth and he fit the leather in between my teeth and cinched the belt around the back of my head.

"Now to get your safeword across," he said, leaning close so it was a whisper in my ear again, "hold your hand up and open and close it. Practice."

Breathing a heavy breath out through my nose since the leather in my mouth made it too difficult to breathe that way, I did what he said, lifting my hand to open and close it.

"Good girl," he said, rubbing a hand over my ass in the way he might a horse's flank. It was both wrong and erotic at the same time, but oh God, *yes*. Nothing was wrong here. Everything was permitted, and my horniness leveled up as I became even slicker between my legs.

He tugged on the belt, pulling my head backwards. "What a good, good little pony you are. I'm gonna ride you now and you're gonna clutch me as tight as you can, little pony. You're going to show me how much you love being ridden and how much you want me to come back to these stables and ride you Every. Single. Day."

I tossed my head, more of a full body shiver, but it made my ponytail swing and Jeremiah smoothed his hand down my ass again. "That's right, girl. You can show me you like my touch. Now give me that flank. Show Master how ready you are for him to ride you."

I thrust my ass out toward him. And I was all but dripping.

There was no world outside this one we were creating in the moment. He was my Master, my rider, and I wanted desperately to be ridden. To know what it would feel like when he mounted me and grasped my reins and took over completely.

And then I felt his cock, long and thick, behind me.

"You're in heat," he growled. "I can smell you. Do you know how hard that makes me? I've been sniffing you out for so long, and now I finally get to mount you and claim you as mine."

His words had me shivering again. "That's right," he said. "Toss your mane all you want. You feel this cock? This cock right here?" He pulled back on the belt at the same time I felt his huge cock against the lips of my pussy.

"You're gonna swallow me down so good with that cunt of yours, aren't you? You're gonna milk this fat horse cock so good till I'm empty, aren't you?"

I couldn't answer, but even if I'd tried, he was tugging back on the reins so my neck was extended backward. Exerting his dominance even as he slowly, and I do mean slowly, torturously, slid his giant cock inside me, stretching and stretching me even though it had only been days ago that I'd last taken him.

I whined and shifted against his entrance and he kept firm pressure on the reins. Not enough to hurt my neck but enough to remind me of who was in control. I bit down on the leather as he filled my body, so big that he was always a strain to fit at first. Would it always be like this, I wondered, half alarmed, half thrilled.

I never wanted this moment to end, I wanted the high of suspended gratification, this lingering first contact before the rush toward climax began.

"Fuck, you're tight as a glove," he swore, pressure releasing on the reins for a moment as both his hands dropped to grip my hips, massaging them as he pushed in deeper still. "You're all woman, aren't you? God, these fucking hips. You're enough to kill a man."

He groaned as he sank all the way in and I could feel his balls against my clit. Still holding my hips, he ground down, rubbing himself all around and giving me friction that had me keening into the leather of the belt.

"That's right, it's a good thing I've got you muzzled." He picked up the reins again and, still balls deep inside me, smacked my ass again. In the after-jiggle, oh my gosh, it felt amazing with him buried inside me and all the—oh, *all* the other bits. I squirmed back against him and he tugged my head backward with the belt.

"Time to ride, baby. Hold on."

I doubted he was joking, so I did. I reached down and grabbed onto the sawhorse.

And Jeremiah started riding. One hand clutching one hip, the other keeping pressure on the reins, he started to fucking ride me. His cock sawed in and out of me, landing with a body-resounding *smack* with each thrust in.

"Ride, pony," he called, "Giddyup." He let go of my hip just long enough to smack my ass. Once, and then again.

And in the moment, I'd never felt more my animal self, giving over to animal pleasures. So when the orgasm rose up at his rough, dominant treatment, I couldn't stop or hold it back and I didn't try to.

It ripped through me like a hurricane and I gave over to it, my muscles shuddering and clamping down.

Jeremiah obviously felt it because he abandoned both reins and the grip on my hips. His arms came around my torso and he hugged me close to him while he rutted me almost crazily from behind.

And I fucking loved every second of it.

I wasn't the only one losing control. He'd locked my arms against myself. I still could have gotten free if I wanted to safeword him, but I didn't want to. He obviously had a thing about people touching him —so as much as I wanted to cling back to him as he thrust wildly and then even more wildly still as his orgasm rose. Then, in a final frantic rush he fucked and fucked me until he finally clutched me harder than ever before and I felt the rush of his release deep inside me.

We were both sweaty now and I'd never felt more intensely connected to another person, even though I was faced away from him.

He started to let go and I shook my head.

"'Ot 'et," I said through the leather gag and he got my meaning by the way I reached for his hands with just a pinky to show I didn't want him to let go of me yet.

So he stayed still several more minutes, him bent over me and arms clasped around me, both of us naked from the waist down, his cock buried deep in me, as we recovered our breaths.

9

Buck

So she was fucking the boss. It was just like that bitch to worm her way back in here.

Buck stayed with his eye pressed against the slat of the stables until his boss finally stood up and pulled his dick out of the bitch, his cum slicking down her legs.

Buck shook his head even as he checked out her ass. Buck preferred his bitches skinnier, but there was no accounting for taste, apparently.

He pulled back from the see-through slat. Nothing to see now and he couldn't get caught. Not now that Ruth was back in his grasp.

It was time to figure out a more permanent solution to his Ruth problem.

Obviously, pouring sugar into her gas tank hadn't done the trick. He'd been hoping to hear about a tragic car accident, but nope, she just kept showing up like a bad penny.

And him, what did he have? He worked sun-up to sundown on

land that shoulda belonged to *him*. But he was nothin' more than an afterthought to these people.

It weren't right.

Things oughta be made right. Even little kids knew that. Things should be fair.

And when they weren't, you had to stand up for yourself and make 'em that way.

10

Jeremiah

It was hard to stop myself from grabbing Ruth as she got dressed again and dragging her back to the sawhorse, or to the ground, or shoving her back up against a wall.

I'd just emptied my balls into her and had barely finished cleaning her up, yet here I was, getting hard all over again.

But the sun was going down and if I didn't show up for dinner with the in-laws, I knew Reece would wring my neck.

"You staying for dinner?" It was out of my mouth before I'd really thought through any implications she might take from me asking.

She looked over at me, her eyes a little wide as she tugged her T-shirt back on over her head. A shame to cover up those perfectly pert, lush breasts of hers held up in a lacy bra that I had to wonder if she wore just for me. Which made my hard-on even stiffer.

She shook her head though, glancing away from me. "It's a big day tomorrow and I should be getting back home."

"Without your car?"

"Charlie's letting me use hers since she's staying here with her parents."

I nodded. "Just make sure you're gassed up."

She rolled her eyes and then sauntered toward me, a saucy smile on her lips. "Yes, *sir*. And same to you."

She was teasing, but she had no clue how much her saying that had me wanting to flip her back over, this time over my lap. Oh yes, I could just imagine how right it would feel to have her ass up and squirming, the heat of her right over my rigid—

I grabbed her by the back of her head, hands gripping her hair, and dragged her in for a hard kiss.

She surrendered and crashed into my chest, her lips yielding to mine.

But then, almost as soon, she was pushing against my chest and pulling back. Goddamn this woman, never fully submissive, always pushing, pushing.

Part of me wanted to pull her back, to master her completely, but the part of my sanity I was still managing to hold onto let her go.

For now, anyway.

But maybe soon I could steal her away for a weekend. And show her what I could do when I really had my leisure. I'd tie her up exquisitely. To keep her exactly where I wanted while I played and explored each part of her at will. At *my* will.

Not now, though.

Now she danced away from me and I had to live with the memory of the taste of her on my lips. But that only made my cock leap, because I hadn't had the taste of her on my tongue, not really yet. And that was a travesty that I would absolutely fix the next time I had her beneath me. I'd latch my arms around those thighs of hers and lock her in place until I memorized the smell and taste of her, and had her screaming my name until she forgot her own...

"See you later, sexy," she said with a cute little wave as she sauntered out of the stable.

I shut my eyes and breathed out hard. When that didn't work, I put a hand down on my hard cock. "Down, boy. You heard the lady. *Later.*"

And I was left to try to walk off my damn stiffy as I cleaned up my work tools and made my way back up to the main house. Charlie's car was gone and I breathed out again, my body finally back under control. *Mostly* anyway. As long as I did not think of a certain curvy red-headed siren who could tempt the saintliest monk. And I was far from saintly. Ha.

I pulled open the door to the house and heard voices from beyond the foyer in the kitchen. Since we'd redesigned the house, we'd made this door the front door since we all used it as one anyway. Except now, instead of opening right into the kitchen, I walked into the foyer. The bottom floor was fairly open concept except for the one-bedroom suite in the back, so even from here I could see everyone congregated in the area off to the side of the kitchen.

We didn't have flooring in here yet, so it was still just a concrete base with basic drywall up on the walls. Hardly the most welcoming, but it was clean, and we'd managed to scrounge up a big picnic table that Charlie had covered with a big plastic gingham tablecloth.

And really, who cared what the table looked like when you had catering from a premiere restaurant in the hill country? Reece had stopped off and gotten the meal earlier, with instructions to reheat and serve. It smelled fucking delicious and I couldn't wait to dig in.

In addition to the rest of the usual ranch chores—which on their own were enough to keep a man working all day—I'd been finishing up restorations on the barn. And that after staying up till an ungodly hour in the morning last night finishing up this place so it'd be not just adequate accommodations for Charlie's parents, but luxury, since apparently, they were some kinda hoity toity who couldn't handle any sorta rough living.

"Oh, look." Reece jumped up from where he was sitting like a damn jackrabbit and started my way. "It's my twin brother I've been talking your ear off about. Jeremiah," he said, clapping me on the back after loping over to me, "come meet Charlie's mom and dad."

I walked forward, my brother's arm heavy around my neck. As I got closer, I was wondering if maybe I should've run by the bunkhouse and changed—especially when Mrs. Winston's nose wrinkled in distaste like she could smell me. Mr. Winston sat beside her, eyes on her instead of me, and it was obvious where he took his cues from.

A weight sank in my stomach.

People used to look at me like this. Like I stank. Like I was street trash it was better for their eyes to skim right past.

"Sorry, it's my bad manners," I said, wiping my hands on my jeans even though they weren't exactly dirty. Well, not in the way this uptight lady imagined. I'd just had them all over Ruth's soft skin.

I looked to Reece. "Why don't I go change and I'll be right back?"

His face was apprehensive, glancing between me and his in-laws, and he gave a sharp nod. "'Kay. Be quick."

But then Charlie stood up, looking appalled. "What? No. You're perfectly fine. Have a seat. We understand you've come in after a hard day at work. Don't we, Mom?"

Her mother held a handkerchief that she'd materialized from somewhere to her nose and shot a glance my way. "Of course," she said in the falsest voice I'd ever heard. "Please. Sit."

Charlie looked mortified as I sat across from her, the furthest away from her mother I could manage.

"I'll serve you up some grub," Reece said with a smile, grabbing my plate from in front of me and hurrying over to the kitchen where the trays of food sat with their tops peeled back.

"So," I looked across the table at Charlie and her parents. "How was the trip? Not too bad, I hope?"

Her mother put the fork she'd been poking at her food with and lifted her nose. "It was absolutely appalling what they've allowed air-travel to become. What happened to the days of customer *service*, that's what I want to know?"

Charlie nodded along, as if a lack of customer service was the real problem with the world.

Mrs. Winston picked up her fork and speared a single pea, and then another and another, until she had five on the tines of her fork, and then she proceeded to eat them without ever letting her lips touch the fork. As if she was preserving her perfect lipstick or something equally ludicrous.

Then she looked over sharply at her husband. "Bernie, for God's sakes, don't play with your food. You know I hate that. Either commit or cover the plate with your napkin."

I watched Bernie to see if he'd tell his wife to fuck off but I had the feeling—

Bernie nodded and picked up his napkin, covering the plate dutifully with it and then putting his hands in his lap.

Yep. It was just what I thought.

I looked down at my food uncomfortably.

I cut into my rosemary chicken. And my hand shook.

No matter how hard I tried, I couldn't bring myself to lift the goddamned bite of chicken to my mouth.

Forcing my eyes shut, I dropped my fork back down to the plate and looked around the table, reaching instead for the glass of wine that had been poured for every place setting. But I swore I felt Mrs. Winston's eyes on my uneaten bite of chicken. Which was fucking ridiculous.

When I tried to key back into the conversation, I could only focus on bits and pieces of what Charlie was rambling on about.

"The boys are doing such impressive work with the ranch... Yield of calves this fall was impressive for taking on the ranch so recently... Jer and Reece are lucky to work so close, they've never been separated their whole lives..."

It wasn't true. Reece and I had been separated for six weeks once.

Six weeks that I never talked about to anybody.

Ever.

"*Bernie*," Mrs. Winston's harsh voice rang out. "Look what you've done now." All eyes at the table zoomed in to watch her spit on her cloth napkin and then start to scrub at his tie where he had dripped some wine.

"I swear," she laughed to everyone else at the table, "I can't take this one anywhere. He'd tie his own shoes together if I wasn't there to help."

Bernie's shoulders slumped as he submitted to his wife's ministrations.

I shot up from the table, taking everyone's gaze off of the humiliated Mr. Winston. "I think I will go get cleaned up after all. I apologize if that means missing the rest of this truly succulent meal." I looked toward Charlie. "Your hospitality, as always, is warm and appreciated. I'll see you tomorrow."

I hoped she could read my sincerity. And also that no one present could sense the slowly rising panic as I turned and all but fled the suffocating room that had suddenly grown full with memories.

Memories of a time I'd tried so very hard to forget.

11

Ruth

Another big day, and one that I didn't imagine I'd be able to find any time to sneak away with a certain hunky twin for forbidden pony play in the stable. Even the memory had me tingling as I met with Charlie and her obnoxious mother for breakfast the next morning. I mean, her father was there, but he faded into the background so much that he may as well not have been, apart from the occasionally cutting comments his wife sent his way. But Charlie just ignored them, so I did too.

Luckily, her mother watched the Today Show religiously because Hoda and Savannah were just her *favorites,* so we were off the hook for a couple hours.

I got started preparing the food for the day in the half-finished kitchen while Charlie napped with her head down on the counter. Poor girl. She'd been running like a chicken with its head cut off for Lord knew how many weeks now. Ever since they'd gotten engaged a month and a half ago.

Yes, six weeks was a fast turnaround for a wedding, but far from impossible. Because look at us, here we were, pulling it off. By the skin of our teeth, maybe, but it was getting done.

While I waited for another mess of biscuits to cook, I put the finishing touches on the big group email itinerary I'd been working on late into the night last night. I read over it for the umpteenth time, then nodded and finally hit *send*.

Charlie's phone buzzed in her pocket but she didn't wake up. Good. She needed the rest. Anyone could see she was run ragged.

"What's the meaning of this?" her mother asked, shoving the door to the kitchen so hard that it cracked into a wall of cabinets.

Charlie's head jerked up from where she'd been resting it on the counter. "What? Where? What is it?"

Her mother scowled at her. "Drool is *most* unattractive in a bride, darling."

Charlie started swiping at her mouth, obviously embarrassed. I put my hands on my hips. "Can I help you with something, *ma'am*?" That ma'am had almost come out something entirely different, but I was still keeping a lid on it. For the moment.

"This itinerary I just received!" Her shriek had me wincing. Jesus, the woman could wake the dead with that voice.

I blinked and smiled. "Yes? I thought you'd be pleased to get notice of the activities for the rest of the week."

She scoffed. "I expected a *usual* itinerary. Spa treatments. Hair appointments. Not— Not *this*." She waved her phone at me.

Out of patience, I reached for the phone but she yanked it back and I shrugged helplessly, looking at Charlie. "I listed out the dates and times for the wedding events. You want spa appointments or hair or whatever... I guess we can find time for those if you want—"

Her mother scoffed in outrage. "I thought I was hiring a competent wedding planner, that's what I *want*."

"Mom," Charlie said, her voice warning, but her mother was on a roll now.

"Not that anyone consulted *me* on what I wanted for my own child's wedding that I am *paying* for. But no, my one and only daughter couldn't have the wedding in civilization where friends and family could attend. She has to be exotic! And have her wedding out in the middle of nowhere, where I'm frankly surprised there's even central plumbing!"

"Well, I guess it's lucky you got here this week and not last one," Reece said as he came in, busting the tension with a big, jovial laugh. "We'd only barely got the main line running and hauled out the construction Port-a-potty over the weekend."

Mrs. Winston's mouth dropped open, clearly appalled, but Reece either didn't notice or played as if he didn't.

"We just caught sight of Xavier's trailer coming up the road," Reece said. "Y'all wanna come out and say hi?" he said, smile still all-American bright.

Yeah, there was definitely no mixing up the two twins. Jeremiah was perpetually stormy and Reece was generally a laid-back guy given to sunshine. He was exactly what Charlie deserved. She'd had enough stormy in her life.

"Absolutely," I said, hooking my arm through Charlie's. "We've always been so curious to meet the great Xavier."

Charlie's mom just waved at us. "I'm feeling a little overheated." She waved at herself rapidly. "I think a hot flash might be coming on. Bernie," she turned and snapped at her husband. "Go get my mini-fan. It's by the bed."

He didn't even nod or voice assent, he just robotically got up from the chair where he'd seated himself and hurried to obey her.

"Fair enough," Reece said. "I'm sure you'll have a chance to meet them later. Just for whenever you do, please remember that Xavier is a vet who was injured overseas. His face was disfigured and people weren't too kind to him at first, so if you please, try not to treat him any different."

Mrs. Winston just huffed. "I would never look down on a former member of the armed forces. How could you ever insinuate that I would?"

"Of course not, ma'am," Reece hurried to say. "I just like to prepare people so they aren't shocked by his face, that's all."

His mother sniffed, obviously not mollified.

I tugged on Charlie's arm to get her away from the toxic drama queen. After meeting her mother it was a wonder she'd turned out as normal and down to earth as she had. Then again, it had taken her a helluva long time to find any kind of healthy in her life.

And I certainly wasn't gonna let her mama rain on her parade now that she had.

We stepped outside just as a huge RV parked and another truck hauling a horse trailer pulled in behind it.

A giant of a man got out from the driver's seat. A woman stepped out of the passenger side, and a passel of kids poured out from the back.

The woman leaned in the back seat and brought out a smaller child, a little older than a toddler, with a pink bow on her head, and held the little girl on her hip as she pulled back out.

Jeremiah intercepted them, coming from the barn, before we could make it out of the house.

I was still too far away to hear what was said, but I could see the little girl bucking to get out of her mom's arms. While Jeremiah shook the man's hand, the little girl rocketed toward us where we were stepping down from the house.

She sprinted toward Reece and leapt at him. He hefted her midair up into his arms. It looked almost choreographed, obviously something they'd done many times before, and her delighted squeals of, "Uncle Weece!" warmed even my cynical heart.

I glanced over at Charlie and just shook my head at the misty-eyed look on her face. "Girl, you are such a goner." I laughed at her.

Then she linked her arm in mine and pulled me forward out of the rest of the group.

Jeremiah looked at us over the man's shoulder. "Here's Ruth, who you bought the property from. And this is Charlie, the woman of the hour who managed to enchant my brother. Ruth, Charlie, this is Xavier."

I was glad for Reece's little reminder inside about Xavier's face. Reece had mentioned his boss had a scarred face before, but I guess I hadn't imagined it was quite as dramatic as it was. The whole left half was quite badly damaged. By fire? I had no idea, but there was obviously some story there.

Charlie smiled and waved hello while I stepped forward with my hand out.

"Hi," I said. "So good to finally meet you in person."

Xavier shook my hand, but he was not smiling. "I have to say, there were times last year when I couldn't imagine ever standing here shaking your hand. You caused my lawyers no end of grief."

I felt my cheeks heat even as his huge giant's hand enveloped mine. "This land was hard to let go of."

He nodded and didn't seem angry. "That's a sentiment I can understand. People don't value their connection to land enough these days. It's my opinion that connecting again to the land is the one thing that might be our salvation in these troubled times. So no, Miss Harshbarger, I don't begrudge you trying to hold onto any part of your family's land. I admire you, even. I hope my sons and daughters connect to the land as deeply as you have."

"Oh," I said, quite shocked that he'd taken my conniving in such an affable way. Jeremiah had tried to explain that his boss had different feelings about land and profits than most folks, but it was infinitely refreshing to see it here up close and personal.

"Now," he smiled, finally letting go of my hand and turning to Charlie, "I hear there's a lovely new young lady to be welcomed into the family." He reached forward and clasped her hand in both of his. "I'm so happy to get to finally meet you and spend a little time with you this week. Reece and his brother have always been special to me. They came to my ranch when I'd barely begun to build it into what it is today."

He grinned at Reece. "Which is why I'm honored to gift you Lightning and Sally Anne as wedding presents today."

Reece's mouth dropped open and his head spun to look at Jeremiah, who was also grinning at him. "You knew?"

Jeremiah shrugged and gave a modest nod.

"You son of a bitch!" he said, but then gave his brother a harsh, rough hug. He let go of him only to turn to Xavier and give him a similarly rough hug full of hard back pats on both sides. Masculine affection at its best.

But when Reece pulled back, his eyes were shining. "Lightning?" He looked at Xavier incredulously. "But he's one of your top-dollar breeders."

Xavier shrugged. "I've got others. And if I ever need him to sire, I expect you'll lend a friend a hand."

"Of course," Reece said, his eyes still wide with shock at the generous present.

"And this way," Jeremiah said, smiling big at his brother, "you can start our own horse breeding program here. To really get your family started on the right foot."

Reece nodded, eyes getting wider and wider as he started to really realize the implications. They could breed and train horses, from what Jeremiah told me about the work they used to do in Montana. It would bring in even more streams of income for the ranch.

I kept my smile plastered on my face even as I glanced away, looking out on the land. The land I'd looked out my bedroom window at every day of my life. I'd always dreamed of running horses out of this place in addition to cattle. The original stables here had been for the hands 'cause back in the day all cowboying had been done from atop a horse and not on a four-by-four. But they'd also stabled Caramel here, the horse I'd ridden and jumped in competitions into high school when they'd had to sell her off to pay the bills.

Ahead, Xavier's two boys had found some long sticks and they were sword-fighting with them. The little toddler girl had picked up a smaller one and was swinging it around, half stumbling and flailing as she did so.

Xavier's wife had come around to us and gave a wave. "Hi, I'm Mel. This wild pack," she gestured at the kids, "belongs to me."

"Mel of Mel's ranch?" Charlie asked, her face lighting up. "Oh my gosh, we've heard so much about you."

"Reece has chatted my ear off about you too, honey," Mel said, holding her arms out big toward Charlie. Charlie grinned and leaned in. The two shared a hug of the sisterhood and I wondered if there'd be a way for me and Charlie to sneak Mel off with our friend Olivia when I remembered, duh, bachelorette party!! We'd find someone to watch the kids. Pawn them off on the mother-in-law, ha! The plan was shaping up in my head better and better.

Why was I letting all this wedding planning get me so down and stressed out? Yeah, theoretically we were trying to make a good impression on Charlie's mom, but I bet no matter what we did, it wasn't going to impress that old hag, so we better make sure not to forget to have some good old-fashioned fun along the way.

"Ladies," I put an arm around each of their shoulders as soon as their hug broke up. "We know that the boys will be boys, but I'm thinking we'll have one last fabulous bachelorette blow-out tomorrow night to celebrate our girl here. How does that sound to y'all?"

Charlie looked surprised. "But there's no bachelorette party on the itinerary."

"That's cause I only made that thing for your mom. No offense," I made a face as I leaned in with a whisper, "but she's not invited. And tomorrow's perfect since it's a day *before* the day before the wedding, so you won't be hungover on your actual wedding day. See, I think of everything." I winked at Charlie, then turned to Mel. "Plus, there's no better way for our new friend to get to know the local wildlife." I waggled my eyebrows at her, then did an in-place salsa. "A little dancing. A little pitcher of margaritas. Or three. We'll stop counting as the night goes on."

Mel laughed. "You must be Ruth?" she asked and I nodded.

"I always knew I was gonna like you girls if we ever met."

"Hell, yeah," I held out my fist. She bumped it and we both grinned.

12

Buck

He sat at the corner of the bar nursing a Bud Lite and watching the women pour in, chattering like magpies. He dropped his face toward his beer but he didn't need to. They were all wrapped up in themselves without a glance to anything or anyone around them.

Yup, that tracked. Ruth Harshbarger always stomped through this world as if it was all hers for the taking, no matter who she fucked over on the way.

He upended the stein of beer in front of him and then signaled for another. He might as well while he had the tab open.

Wasn't like he could afford to close it after his run of shit luck at the card tables over in Austin last night. He'd been so sure his ace high was enough to close that goddamned hand. How the fuck was he supposed to have guessed that the fucker beside him was going to pull out pocket kings at the last minute? That was some bullshit, but no one would listen when he bellowed that the guy was cheating, and *he'd* been the one they'd thrown out.

He shook his head and took the full stein that was replaced in front of him. He might as well enjoy this last night out before they cut up his damn Visa.

He took a long swig and glared across the bar at the bitch who was the cause of his every misfortune.

If not for her, he'd be a rich man right now.

He'd be wealthy, a man of stature. A man no one would ever toss out like yesterday's trash. No, instead they'd be shitting themselves to get out of *his* way, to roll out the red carpet for him. *That* was the life he'd deserved.

And the scales had been out of balance for long enough. Things should be *fair*. She didn't just get to ride off into the sunset when he — When everything was—

He took another long swallow of beer. He'd stopped tasting it a long time ago. And damn, he had to fuckin' piss.

But after that—after that he was gonna give that bitch what was comin' to her. It was her fault it had come to this, not his. A man could only be pushed so far. A man could only be pushed so far.

13

Ruth

"A toast!" I called out, loud enough to be heard above the pumping country music, lifting my beer up. The four of us—Charlie, our other best friend Olivia, and Mel were all seated at a table off to the side of the dance floor, as far away from the speakers as we could get. "To Charlie. Olivia and I will always be your best friends, through thick and thin, in sickness and in health, amen!"

Olivia giggled. "Those are wedding vows, not a toast."

"Friendships are more important than marriages, everybody knows that."

Charlie thought about it for a moment, then nodded and lifted her glass of vodka soda to clink my beer bottle.

I grinned and turned to Melody. "And to new friends. Welcome to the posse."

"The pussy posse!" Olivia sputtered out a huge laugh, and then covered her mouth. "Oh shit," she giggled. "I think I'm drunk."

"Since when do you outdrink me?" I asked. "And clank your damn bottle so I can put my arm down."

She lifted her bottle and finished the toast, "To friends near and far."

"To friends near and far," we all intoned and then tipped our heads back and took swigs of our various drinks.

"Okay, so what's the scoop?" Charlie asked, patting her hand on the table in Melody's direction. "What were Reece and Jeremiah like back when they lived at your ranch?"

I leaned in, ready for all the gossip.

But Melody was annoyingly retrospect. She just shook her head and grinned. "These are *my* boys we're talking about here. I came to get to know y'all."

Charlie arched an eyebrow. "To make sure I'm good enough for him?"

Melody kept her easy smile but didn't say no.

"But Charlie's the best!" Olivia said, eyes wide. "Everybody thinks so. I bet even Jeremiah is bummed his brother snatched her up first."

"Ew, God, no," Charlie said, tossing a napkin at Olivia, at the same time I shuffled in my chair, sitting up straighter.

I know people had fantasies about twins and all, but I was glad that Reece and Jeremiah were the kind who kept strict boundaries when it came to their love lives.

Though apparently that wasn't the case of everyone who lived back at the ranch they'd come from, because as the hours went on, we all opened up, even Mel.

"So wait," Olivia said, eyes wide. "There's a woman that lives on your ranch and she's got two fellas…"

Mel nodded wryly. "Two partners, yes." It had become apparent throughout the evening that she liked shocking Olivia.

Olivia sat back and fanned her hand at her face rapidly, her cheeks getting pink. "Well, I can't say as I ever thought about that." She was quiet another moment, staring out into the crowd before muttering as if she'd forgotten we were even there. "But I guess with the right guys, it doesn't sound half bad…"

Charlie let out a bleat of laughter. "Honey, you can barely handle it when you have *one* guy on the hook. Imagine trying to handle two at once."

Olivia shuddered. "Oh my God, you're right." Still, by the look on her face, I could tell she was still thinking the idea over. I just shook my head. It wasn't like I was one to talk. No, I wasn't taking on two lovers at once, but sneaking around with Jeremiah—it was certainly playing with fire.

I couldn't rid myself of the feeling that Mel had her eyes on me all night, like she could sense something was going on between me and Jeremiah. It was clear she'd taken on a sort of motherly role toward all the men who'd lived on her husband's ranch even though she was barely in her mid-thirties. I guess when you had little ones running around, maybe it came more naturally?

Mel seemed like a superstar to me. She had her shit so together, she was this superstar mom, and it was clear she and her husband were still disgustingly in love even after all these years together...

God, in comparison, I was a total mess. I bet when she was my age, she had things so much more figured out.

I was twenty-five and *still* barely had a direction in life or an idea of what I was gonna do when I grew up, much less any roots down anywhere. I'd be starting all over from scratch when I moved to Fort Worth. And yeah, sometimes uprooting and moving worked out like it had for Charlie, but I knew those were rare odds. And as the daughter of a gambling addict, I knew better than to bet on long odds.

And suddenly, in the middle of this bright, loud party, I felt melancholy.

All this would be going away. The camaraderie. The friends. Being able to go to a bar where I recognized faces and names. Where I had a place.

I'd been telling myself this was all a bonus of moving on—because people recognized me back, and here I would always be Ruth Harshbarger, the girl whose dad fucked up royally and screwed over half the town by running up debts.

In a new place I'd have a blank slate, something I'd never experienced before.

But blank slates were exactly that... Blank.

You had to build everything from scratch. And making friends as an adult was *hard*. During the period where everyone had cut me off before I'd been able to pay people back after selling the ranch, I'd been friendless and it had been a cold and lonely time. I'd always just taken friends for granted. But then they suddenly weren't there anymore... except for Olivia. She had a busy life of her own, though, and there had been a lot of cold and empty nights alone on the ranch until the boys and Charlie came, bringing life with them.

But before that—I hadn't known a loneliness quite so empty as being on that ranch in winter without a soul to talk to and no one to call. And with nowhere to go where I'd be welcome.

It would be different this time, though. I'd get to know people. I could be social and come out of my shell with people I didn't know.

I looked over at Charlie, grinning and taking slow sips of her vodka, which was again running low. She was listening to Mel tell another story about the guys on the ranch, how apparently one of them, a guy named Liam, just *loved* playing pranks on everybody else.

So when they'd hired a new guy on to take up some of the slack from Reece and Jeremiah leaving, apparently Liam decided it was time for one of his infamous pranks.

"He would not let up on this guy," Mel continued. "Saran wrap across his door in the morning. Putting just enough stuffing in the toe of his boots so they didn't fit right, but it wasn't obvious. No one would fess up. So Blue, the new guy, is getting more and more pissed. But Liam's not about to let up. And he's *also* been pretending to be an American this whole time, like he's not Irish."

"And what does your husband say to all this?"

"Xavier stays out of it. As long as the guys put in their hours and don't give him trouble, he leaves them be. But Blue did start noticing that our kids laughed whenever they were nearby and Liam spoke with an American accent. He thought it was another prank and it was, but he couldn't figure it out. It was driving the poor guy nuts."

"So what happened?" Charlie asked. "Did he ever get a clue?"

Mel's grin was slow. "Oh yeah, I'd say he did. Since he didn't know who was doing it all, he decided to take his revenge on all of them, all at once."

"It started in the morning, with donuts. He brought a separate box for me and the kids, but the one for the guys? All jelly-filled donuts. Except they were special. He'd also piped some ketchup into them. Most of the guys spit them out, all except for Liam who ate all of his and said it was delicious."

Olivia was laughing her ass off, hiccupping from the alcohol and the story.

I backed away from the table. "I'll go get another round."

"But you have to hear how the story finishes!" Olivia cried.

"I've grown up around men my whole life," I said with a laugh. "I can imagine. So that's two Fat Tires and a vodka soda, yeah?"

Mel and Olivia nodded but Charlie reached out and grabbed my forearm. "Just tell them mine is for the bride-to-be. They'll know what I mean."

I nodded but frowned after I turned away. What did she mean by that? I went to the bar and gave my order, repeating the words Charlie had told me to say. The bartender nodded knowingly and several minutes later gave me a little cardboard carrier with the drinks to carry back.

On impulse, after I'd turned back toward the table, I paused and looked down at the cup of vodka soda. I took one glance toward the table where the girls were sitting. They were all still laughing and fully absorbed. So I picked up the vodka and took a small sip.

There were the bubbles of the soda... but no vodka in the drink.

My head jerked back up to look at the table.

Oh shit.

No, no, no, I didn't need to go jumping to conclusions. Maybe she just didn't want to get smashed the night *before* the night before her wedding?

But I'd never seen Charlie hold back before.

Either way, I had to know. I was moving away, for God's sake. And if there was some other reason...

I stalked back to the table, set the drink tray down on the table, and hooked my arm around Charlie's as I leaned over to speak directly in her ear. "Why are you pretending to drink vodka when you aren't really?"

I pulled back and looked in her face and I saw it there plain as day. "Oh my God, you're pregnant," I whispered, and then clapped a hand over my mouth.

Charlie's eyes went wide as saucers and she shot back in her seat.

"You are?" Olivia squealed. "Oh my God, why didn't you tell us? Congratulations!" She almost fell over herself as well as Mel, jumping up and leaning across the table to try to hug Charlie. All she managed to accomplish was tipping over the two very full beers I'd just put down.

"Jesus!" I swore and barely managed to grab the bottlenecks right as they started pouring brown liquid all over the table and Charlie was stepping back even more, shaking her head back and forth.

"No one's supposed to know," she said, so quietly I more read her lips than heard her above the loud music. "Not until after."

Her hand went to her tummy, which was still flat as far as I could see.

I nodded. Having gotten to know her mom and how judgmental she was, I could get it. And maybe it was really early along, maybe they'd just found out—

"How far along?" Olivia asked excitedly, all but bouncing on her feet.

Charlie's eyes bounced furtively among the group. "Three months."

My mouth dropped open; I couldn't help it. She was three months pregnant and she hadn't told me? We lived together and were best friends. At least I thought we were.

"Is that why you're getting married so fast?" Olivia asked, and my head swung around toward her. Jesus, she really was drunk. She usually had more tact, but it was true when she was drunk, she would just say whatever was on her mind. It had ruined more than one relationship—when she got drunk and told her boyfriends what she really thought of them. I'd been grateful in most of those cases, but now I was really wishing we'd *all* been drinking vodka sodas minus the vodka tonight.

My eyes came back to Charlie right as a raucous country song started over the speakers and a whoop came from the crowd as people around us flooded to the dance floor.

"Bathroom break," Charlie said. "Come on."

"I'll stay and keep the table," Mel said.

Charlie looked at her gratefully while Olivia and I followed her toward the back of the bar and into the women's restroom. Closing the door behind us provided a modicum of quiet compared to the roar of the music beyond.

"Okay," I said. "Spill."

Charlie looked at both of us, anxiety on her face as she wrung her hands. "I didn't mean to hide it from y'all. It's just, Reece and I thought it would be best to keep the news to ourselves."

I frowned. "I can get not wanting to tell your mom, but—"

Charlie shook her head. "It's not just that. Reece always worries what his brother thinks of him. He feels like Jeremiah only just stopped thinking of him as a fuck-up. But getting me knocked up and having to throw a shotgun wedding—"

"But you love him, right?" Olivia asked.

"Oh God, yes, I do, I really do! Our timeline might have gotten a little... well, moved up because of the baby, but I'm seriously the happiest I've ever been in my whole life."

It reflected in her face too. When she smiled, it lit behind her eyes.

Her hands went to her stomach. "And to have a baby on top of it all..." Her voice trailed off as her eyes grew shiny and her smile grew even wider. "It's a miracle."

"Oh, honey," I said, and threw my arms around her. "I couldn't be happier for you."

She hugged me back. "Really? You don't think we're being reckless?"

I laughed as I pulled back. "Anyone who tells you life goes according to set plans are full of BS. But you do realize that Jeremiah can do math. When this baby pops out three months early, he's going to put two and two together."

She shrugged. "We figure by then he'll be too enamored with the idea of being an uncle and we'll already be married, proving we're mature and handling everything. Reece is an amazing man and I hate that his brother can't see that."

"I don't know. Jeremiah's been letting up on him lately, hasn't he?" I asked.

Charlie shrugged. "A little, I guess. He's just been *big brother* for too long. He doesn't know how to relax and let go, you know?"

Oh, I knew. That man had a control problem. Granted, I happened to enjoy that little quirk of his. But only for a few more days, and then I was out of here.

Which meant I'd only get to see the new baby on visits when I was able to get enough time off to come down. My heart sank.

If this was the time for confessions, I ought to open up and tell Charlie I was leaving.

But I was clearly a coward, because as Olivia cooed over the baby and pressed her hand against Charlie's stomach, I just stood there silent and still as a scarecrow.

I told myself it was Charlie's day and I didn't want to detract from it, but maybe I was just still in denial myself. This was where I wanted to be. These people were my family. I hated that there wasn't a place for me here.

Oh God, was that what I was doing sleeping with Jeremiah? Was sleeping with him my desperate last gasp at holding on to this life?

"Come on," Olivia said, grasping Charlie's hand and jumping up and down. "Now we have even more reasons to celebrate. Let's go dance!"

Charlie laughed but then her eyes went wide and she pulled her hand back. "First, I gotta pee. Oh my God, they weren't kidding about the being pregnant and needing to pee every five seconds thing. And I'm not even showing yet!"

She hurried off into a stall while Olivia pulled a makeup kit out of her purse and started refreshing herself. I could only sort of stare off into space. A *baby*. Charlie was going to have a baby. I don't know why it blew my mind so much, but it did.

But then Charlie was back and Olivia was stuffing her makeup kit back in her purse and then I was reaching for the bathroom door.

As soon as I opened though, I let out a little shriek of surprise at who was standing on the other side.

"What are *you* doing here?"

14

Buck

I watched on from the other side of the bar in disgust as the women's damn knights in shining armor showed up. The women had all flocked like women do to the bathroom and I thought I mighta had my chance to snatch Ruth out from among them.

But no, right at that exact moment, Reece, Jeremiah, and that big, deformed bastard visiting for the week all swept in, stopped by the table, and then the twins angled toward the restrooms, surprising the girls as they came out.

Which just fucking steamed him. Cutting him off from his quarry again, right when he'd psyched himself up to finally take action.

What was he gonna do now? Keep waiting? Waiting for fucking what? For the world to end? His was falling down all around him as he sat here. He had no more fucking money and with another missed payment, they were gonna repo his damn truck.

He staggered off his chair and wove through the crowd toward the exit. Think. *Think.* He pounded on the side of his head as he wove and stumbled down the sidewalk toward his truck.

There had to be some way to make it all right.

To make it *fair*. It couldn't be too late. It was never too late.

Fuck, his head was bleary. It was hard to think straight.

Tomorrow. He'd figure it all out tomorrow.

And then she'd pay.

He'd make her pay.

It was the last thought he had as he yanked open his door, dropped into the back seat, and passed out.

15

Jeremiah

I woke up only a little bit bleary-eyed the next morning. I hadn't had much to drink last night at the bar with the women, but I knew I was the only one.

They'd all been well on their way to blotto by the time we'd shown up. Well, Charlie had looked pretty steady on her feet, but after we got there, I never saw her without a vodka soda in her hand. Olivia giggled every time she got a new one, but then that girl was three shots past blasted.

Neither Reece or I was super comfortable with the thought of the girls out barhopping without anyone there to watch out for them, and it turned out Xavier had even stronger feelings on the subject when his wife was involved, so it was inevitable we'd ended up crashing their party.

And it was fun.

Although seeing Ruth in that tight, revealing little number she'd been wearing last night and keeping my hands off her had been difficult.

Ever since we'd begun... whatever it was we were doing... well, it just seemed *wrong* for her to be close and for me not to be able to put my hands on her.

And every time she danced with some other asshole there, right in front of me as if to spite me, I wanted to yank her away from him and slam her up against the wall to remind her exactly how well I could satisfy her and satisfy her so completely she could forget the face of any other man she'd ever met.

But considering my brother and future sister-in-law, not to mention our *boss* and his wife were right there, I'd had to cage my more caveman-like urges.

Meanwhile, Ruth just kept dancing and grinning and apparently having a grand old time, like she knew she was taunting me and was loving doing so. From the wicked little smiles she flashed my way when no one else was looking, I would have guessed it was a performance all for my benefit.

Which just made my hand twitchy for her backside.

Not that I was able to get my palm anywhere near said backside, because she just winked at me as she sent Charlie home with us and took an Uber home with Olivia.

At least I wasn't the only one hard up. I smirked over at my brother sprawled on the cot across from my bed. He was drooling all over his pillow, arm off the cot, dragging on the floor.

"Hey, asshat," I said, tossing my pillow at him. "Up and at 'em."

He jerked up when my pillow hit him, looking around in alarm. When he saw it was just me, he grabbed the pillow I'd thrown at him, shoved it under his head, mumbled, "Five more minutes," and slumped back down.

I rolled my eyes, then took pity on him.

I'm sure he would have liked to have gotten up close and personal with Charlie last night considering how they were cemented to each other on the dance floor.

Too bad Charlie's mom was waiting up for us all to come home last night. She hurried Charlie in the house and glared at Reece for getting her baby home so late. I'd almost busted up laughing in my brother's bereft face right in front of the in-laws.

I don't know where they'd been planning to sneak off to, but the mother-in-law had definitely put the kibosh on those plans.

Probably for the best, considering that had been about four hours ago and now it was time to be up and at 'em.

I walked over to my brother and yanked the pillow out from under his head. "Five minutes are up."

He groaned. "*Noooooooo.*"

"Yes," I said. "Now get your ass outta bed. It might be the day before your wedding, but you live on a ranch and there's shit to do. Come on, we gotta get the feed out."

Reece gave one more groan of protestation but, unlike when he was younger, he didn't keep on whining and complaining. He got up and, still only half awake, climbed into his jeans and shrugged on a shirt and boots.

We went about our morning chores feeding the cattle and horses, then headed in for breakfast.

Charlie looked frazzled as she cooked scrambled eggs in the bunkhouse kitchen while pancakes sizzled on a side griddle. Her eyes shot immediately to Reece as we came in. "Thank God, you're back. I think I might just strangle my mom if I'm left alone with her any longer."

Reece immediately went over and took over cooking the eggs. "Sit, sit," he said, gently kissing the side of her head. "I got this."

I paused in the doorway, watching the two of them. I had to admit, he was good with her. It was like meeting her had been the last kick in the pants to grow up. After years begrudging my trouble-maker brother, maybe he really had finally settled down and become the man I always hoped he could be.

And if he was a grown man and not my immature little kid brother who needed watching after anymore…

All I'd ever known was the two of us, scraping and fighting against the world.

But watching Reece and Charlie, I could see what they were building, their own little unit, the two of *them* against the world.

It was a good thing. And if I was feeling a little displaced… I took a step back from the doorway, but Reece turned to me.

"Jer, can you get the big tray? We'll need to carry all this up to the big house so we can have breakfast with the in-laws. You gotta come too, 'cause the more people, the more buffer we can give Char from her mom."

"Sure thing," I said, but even as I went forward, I couldn't help thinking, whoa, whoa, whoa, since when was my little brother the one giving orders around here?

But I just loaded up a tray with the large stack of pancakes and bottle of syrup. Reece covered the pan of eggs and Charlie carried plates as we all trekked back over to the big house.

Charlie's mother was not impressed by the fair provided, naturally.

"Well, I usually prefer crêpes but I *suppose* I can make an exception." She looked sharply up at Charlie. "Is it vegan? You know I'm strictly eating vegan lately."

"Absolutely," Charlie said straight-faced, even though I'd seen the mix she'd used and doubted it was.

I also doubted that her mother understood what "vegan" meant since she spooned some of the fluffy eggs onto her plate.

The silence around the breakfast table was painful. Her father read the Austin American Statesman; he must have picked up a copy yesterday in town? I just chowed down and watched my brother and Charlie occasionally attempt awkward conversation that was quickly shot down by the Dragoness-in-Chief.

"After breakfast I'm going to go pick up Ruth so we can finish getting everything ready for the rehearsal dinner tonight," Charlie said.

Her mother made a disgruntled face as she looked toward her daughter. "I thought the point of hiring a wedding planner was so that you didn't have to think of any last-minute plans. It's supposed to be *your day*."

I knew Charlie well enough to know she was *barely* holding back an eye roll. Instead, she forced a smile through her teeth. "Yes, but I *want* to be involved, and Ruth is one of my best friends. I think it's fun to be involved."

Her mother wiped daintily at the corners of her mouth with a napkin. "Well, one might think you'd want to spend what little time you have with your mother since we so rarely get to see one another anymore. I mean, my God, you move out here in the middle of nowhere. You don't call, you don't write, you just disappear, and I have no *idea* where my own flesh and blood is—"

"Well, now you do, Mom," Charlie said, the edge on her voice starting to show. "So now we can visit each other whenever we want. Reece and I can come visit you and Dad in California—"

"Oh, do you mean it?" Her mom's hands shot across the table as she grasped Charlie's hands. "Because we'd love to have you back in our time zone. This whole adventure out west has been... a lark. But it's time for you to come home now. I'm sure all your friends would welcome"—her eyes flitted to my brother—"your new man."

"My *husband*," Charlie corrected. "After tomorrow, he'll be my husband."

I didn't miss the distasteful look that crossed Mrs. Winston's face at the word. It was almost enough to have me pushing back from the table and slamming my napkin down.

It was so clear that these people thought they were better than us, my brother and me. They might as well just come out and say that they thought we were poor white trash. What galled me is that they weren't even wrong. What else could you call yourself when your own *mother* didn't want you? When I'd done plenty I wasn't proud of over the years to get by?

But to sit here and have this sanctimonious woman look down her nose and sneer at my brother as not good enough—

I shoved another big bite of pancakes in my mouth to keep from saying anything. Apparently, that was an uncouth way of eating, though, because Mrs. Winston's eyes came my way and then quickly averted away, the corners of her mouth twitching down again in disgust. I smiled, dug another big bite around in what syrup was left on my plate, and then shoved an even bigger bite in my mouth. My lips barely closed around it, and my cheeks were stuffed with pancakes as I chewed.

"Yes, well. You know your father could find a temporary position for him at his corporation while he attended night classes to get some sort of degree. Then I'm sure we could help him move up the ladder in no time."

"But he works here," I said, mouth still stuffed with pancake.

Charlie looked distressed as her eyes ping-ponged between us and Reece held his hands up. "Charlie—"

"Charlotte," her mother cut in, eyes cold. "Her name is Charlotte."

"*Charlotte* and I," Reece acquiesced, far more patient than I woulda been with this lady, "are happy where we are. We'll be glad to visit but we're making a good home here."

Charlie smiled at him and looked grateful, but his answer certainly wasn't winning him any points with his mother-in-law to be.

"Well," she said tightly, clutching her coffee cup with a white-knuckled grip. "I'm sure we can talk more and settle things after the wedding. You're right, we should just focus on one thing at a time. And tomorrow is your special day." She reached out a hand and caressed Charlie's cheek. "My baby, getting married."

It might have even been a sweet moment, if her mom hadn't proceeded to sigh and drop her hand while murmuring under her breath, "*again*."

Reece wrapped up breakfast pretty quickly after that and trundled Charlie off to go pick up Ruth. He really was a good partner, buffering Charlie like that and getting her away from her terrible mother as quickly as possible.

I watched with arms crossed from outside the house, near what would eventually be a wraparound porch, as my brother helped Charlie in the car and gave her a kiss before sending her off.

Xavier and his family were gone for the day to see Pedernales Falls—one of the many great natural water features in the area from the spring-fed rivers in Central Texas. There were lots of rocks for the boys to jump into the river from and even the younger ones could have fun splashing in the water on the beachy shore.

The rains had moved on and it would get into the high nineties by the afternoon. Ruth would be happy—the forecast called for the sunny weather to continue on for the rest of the week, so the outside ceremony tomorrow should be able to go off without a hitch.

We were having the ceremony back behind the rebuilt house underneath a big oak tree that survived last year's storm. The twister *just* barely bypassed the huge tree, even though ten feet to the left, it had carved up the earth, including the Harshbarger family ranch house that had stood there for a hundred years.

I walked over to my brother after he sent his bride-to-be off to pick up Ruth and clapped a hand on his back. "Come on, little brother, let's go for a ride."

Reece looked at me, eyebrows up in surprise. "Where? I thought we had to—"

I dragged him forward a few steps, my arm firm around his shoulders until he jerked away from my rough grip.

"Hey, asshole, you can't kidnap me the day before my wedding. Where you taking me?"

I rolled my eyes. "Don't be so dramatic, prima donna." I held up my hands. "By all means, go ahead back inside and do some more bonding with the in-laws."

That had him freezing in his tracks. He only had to take one quick glance back at the house before he was in-step beside me. "What'd you have in mind, big brother?"

I laughed and clapped him on the back again, so hard he stumbled a step. Hey, I didn't make the rules—brotherly love had never been the gentle or ooey-gooey kind between us. We'd been kicked out of plenty of foster homes for *rough housing*, which could get so intense occasionally one or the other of us would come away with a bloody nose. Turned out it was good practice for when we ended up on the streets and learned to fight back-to-back, fists out, to the world that always seemed to have it out for us.

We were the only one each other'd had for the longest time. Yeah, things had changed some when we'd found Xavier and he'd taken us in and given us the only family we'd ever known beyond each other.

But this was different. Reece was getting married. Tomorrow he'd be made one with Charlotte. Maybe one day, hopefully a long fucking time from now, they'd even have kids. Fuck, I couldn't imagine Reece as a dad, he was only just now beginning to act like an adult instead of the fuck up I'd had to watch out for and get out of scrapes his whole life. But someday. Starting tomorrow, he was starting a family unit that was separate from me. And it was good. That was the way it was supposed to be.

As we approached the stables, Mike emerged with one of the roan mares Xavier had brought, all saddled.

"Got 'em ready for you, boss," Mike said.

Reece looked at me, again perplexed.

I shrugged. "I figure the day before my little brother gets married, maybe we could take one last ride, just the two of us. Us against the world. And I can give you your wedding present in private."

Reece looked not only surprised but moved, if the way his jaw working and him swallowing was any tell. I rolled my eyes again and slammed him on the shoulder. It shoved him to the side a bit. "Now outta my way. You're riding Sally Anne here and I'm taking Lightning."

"Hey, why do you get the stallion? They were *my* wedding presents!"

I laughed and looked at him over my shoulder. "Yeah, but Xavier says he's barely broke and it'd be *my* ass if I got you thrown the day before your wedding. Plus," I said before disappearing into the stables to find Lightning, "I get dibs cause I'm the oldest."

16

Jeremiah

I sat gingerly at the rehearsal dinner chair that evening.

"I told you, you shoulda let me ride Lightning instead of you," Reece said with a big-ass grin from across the table. We were all out at a fancy restaurant terrace on Lake Travis—they'd had a late cancellation that Ruth managed to snatch for us.

I grimace-smirked an acknowledgement in my brother's direction. "Yeah, yeah. If you'd been on Lightning when he bucked like that, you'd have ended up with a broken ass instead of just a bruised one. I am the master of the tuck and *roll*."

Reece laughed and looked out on the table of our gathered friends and family. "Yeah, more like the master of the awkward fall-and-holler-your-ass-off."

"Hmm, and yet," I undid the cufflinks and shoved up the sleeves of my dress shirt. "Not a scratch." My legs were ripped up all to hell and my tailbone hurt so bad I was trying my hardest to lean forward and put most of the weight of sitting on my thighs, but no one needed to know that.

I grinned. "Plus, I got right back up on that—" *fucker*. I stopped myself just in time and glanced to the right where I saw Charlie's mom reaching for her pearls as if to start clutching them, "that *horse*. So all's well that ends well." I sat back a little without meaning to and struggled not to wince through my smile.

We'd had a great time on the ride, other than the tumble from Lightning when I'd challenged Reece to a race. And the racing wasn't because I was a testosterone-filled jackass who always had to prove his superiority to his twin brother anymore—no, it wasn't because of that. I challenged Reece to race and tried my fucking hardest to beat him because I was intentionally being *nostalgic* for those times.

And if Lightning wasn't exactly on the same page as me and bucked me off when I tried nudging him a little too fervently in his hind quarters—well, I was just chalking that up to an excellent learning experience for all involved.

Plus, giving my little brother the win like that on the day before his wedding was really just the gentlemanly thing to do.

It was nice for all of us to be sitting down like this. Especially when Ruth had done us all a solid by putting the parents-in-law at the opposite end of the table by some of her parents' old friends she'd wrangled into coming. Ruth and Charlie had been on the go all day and after Reece and my brief hour trail ride, so had we.

Ruth's to-do list wasn't endless—it *had* been doable. But only barely.

But Charlie had grabbed her friend's hand and dragged her to sit down and enjoy the actual meal with us. That had been about half an hour ago and we'd all been eating good food, and more importantly, drinking fucking fabulous wine. I wasn't usually a wine guy. I was a hefeweizen guy all day long. But fuck if this cabernet—or whatever the hell this ruby red magic drink was—didn't go down smooth after the fourth or fifth glass. I'd lost track—I just knew the waiters at this fancy as fuck place never let my glass get more than half empty before they were there topping me off.

I felt loose and magnanimous—two words that were usually much more often ascribed to Reece than me. I was the uptight twin.

The stuffy one with a stick up my ass. I knew that was what people thought of me, but tonight I didn't give a fuck.

It felt like this afternoon I'd finally cleared the air with Reece, maybe once and for all.

Reece hadn't even laughed when I'd gotten thrown—he'd immediately jumped off Sally Anne to make sure I was okay, and when he'd reached down a hand to help me up, I'd clasped it in confidence.

Yes, after he'd made sure I was alright, he had hopped back up on his horse and continued the race, finishing long before me since I'd finally decided safety was the better part of valor and took it slow, getting to know our new stallion rather than put my neck on the line again.

But when I finally caught up to Reece at the ridgeline, he wasn't smug. No, he was in one of his rare contemplative moods, staring out at the vast vista of the Texas plane, wheat-colored Bermuda grass as far as the eye could see. It was almost time to harvest again.

"You know," he said, hand loosely on the pommel of his saddle, "I don't know if I ever told you how grateful I am that you decided to drag me along on this little adventure of yours."

"What are you talking about? It's both of ours."

I'd brought my horse right up beside his and he looked over at me with a *yeah, really?* expression. He shook his head. "No way Xavier would've trusted me with this much responsibility on my own. Hell, *I* wouldn't've trusted me."

"Well." I held the reins loosely as we looked out on the sloping hills that seemed to go on forever, huge wide Texas sky overhead. "A lot can change in a year. Moving down here, taking on the ranch—"

Reece laughed. "C'mon, we both know it was Charlie that made the difference. I hate to be one of those men who needed a good woman to turn him around. And I was trying before she got here. I don't know if you'll believe that, but I really was working on my shit. But she just..." He'd trailed off. "She gave me a *reason* for it to stick, ya know? The future wasn't just this hazy *maybe someday* anymore. And I know you don't believe it'll stick, but I swear—"

I shook my head, "No, no, man. I'm sorry I gave you such shit about it at the beginning. I can see it. You have changed. I'm sorry I was holding onto the past like that. You and Charlie are something special. It's why I wanted to bring you out here. I'm proud of you, man. I know I've given you a harder time than anyone, but I'm proud of the man you've become."

I reached into my pocket and pulled out a small box. "It's why I wanted to give you this today." I handed it over to him.

Reece's brow scrunched. "What is it?"

"Open and find out."

He took the box and his big fingers fumbled, but he finally managed to tear the brown paper I'd taped around it and pulled out the simple gold cardboard box inside. He cracked it open.

Reece's eyes immediately shot up to me in surprise. "Holy shit, how do you have this?"

"I kept hold of it since it was the only thing we had left of her."

Reece gingerly lifted our mother's tiny gold locket out of the box. "How? You're telling me you had this the *whole* time? Even when we were broke in San Fran? You never pawned it?"

I swallowed and looked away from him. "I always took care of us, didn't I? We never starved. A family is supposed to have heirlooms to pass down." I shrugged. "And it's just gold-plated. Don't get too excited, it's probably not worth much."

"Well, Jesus, I'm not gonna sell it now, I'm just saying!"

"I thought you could give it to Charlotte."

He nodded and gently dropped it back into the little box. "It'll mean so much to her." He looked up into my eyes. "It means a lot to me. Jesus, even more knowing you held onto it considering everything..." He'd trailed off and then met my eyes again.

"Will you finally tell me what happened during the six weeks you disappeared?"

I closed my eyes and took another long swig of wine. No need to replay that part of the day. Wasn't anything to say about it anyway. I shut Reece down like I always did whenever he ever brought it up, turned my horse around and said we needed to get back because the women would be back soon. I'd been right, too, because as soon as we'd finished brushing down the horses, Charlie had pulled in with Ruth in tow.

The rest of the day had been a whirlwind, getting the chairs delivered and stored in an unfinished room of the house, putting together the platform where the ceremony would be performed, helping the big tent guys get it out of the truck and up, lining out where the chairs would be staged, and finally, doing the rehearsal run through of the ceremony.

Tomorrow I'd be walking down with Ruth on my arm as one of Charlie's bridesmaids, but today I'd just walked with Olivia since Ruth had still been busy working on some finishing touch or other. But still, it had been special standing beside my brother watching on as Charlie held a cluster of rolled newspapers as a stand-in for her flowers, two-stepping down the makeshift 'aisle' they'd marked out on the grass on her father's arm. I swore I'd never seen Charlie grinning bigger than when she'd walked that aisle toward my brother.

I'd looked out and seen in the waning sunlight that even Ruth had stopped her nonstop running around to watch them run through the ceremony. Xavier was officiating—he'd done the online certificate thing, and to hear the big man's voice booming out the wedding vows, followed by Charlie's sweet voice and then my brother's… Well, it was enough to even get to me. And I usually considered myself the least sentimental bastard on earth.

But watching my brother gaze with the most sincerity I'd ever seen on his face as he stared into his woman's eyes—it hit me. Hit me deep.

And then we'd all loaded up and headed into Austin and this posh restaurant that I knew was mostly for Charlie's parents than for anyone else. If it had just been us, we woulda likely had the rehearsal dinner somewhere like the Salt Lick, one of the most famous BBQ places in the hill country. Somehow, I didn't think finger-lickin' good BBQ would have appealed to the pretentious Mrs. Winston's standards. Ruth had still booked them to cater the wedding tomorrow though, cause she knew what real Texas folks expected at a wedding, no matter how supposedly "posh." She'd also contracted with a local tearoom to have cucumber sandwiches. The woman knew how to cover her angles.

I had to say, Ruth was an impressive woman, and I wasn't just saying that about the way she'd been captivating me carnally lately. It was half the damn reason I couldn't get her outta my damn head. A pretty face and a tight body were fairly a dime a dozen. But a woman of quality, who challenged you in and out of the bedroom... or the truck cab as it were...

Fuck, my pants were getting tight under the elegant tablecloth just remembering. My eyes drifted across the table to the siren in question. She was seated across from me, sitting there beside Charlie. The two of them had their heads together and were giggling about something, but Ruth caught me looking at her, and if it was possible, her cheeks went even rosier.

Goddammit, she was the most stunning woman I'd ever seen in my entire life. Like, kudos to my brother and all, but Charlie didn't hold a candle to Ruth's vivacious firecracker energy. She was so full of *life*.

It had been hard to keep my hands off her all day. Only being busy myself and knowing she barely had a second to spare as it was had kept me away. But now, feeling so loose, and watching the way her hair shone under the lights of the sconces, and hearing her bell-like laughter ring out every few moments from something Olivia or Charlie said...

I pushed back from my chair as the servers brought out dessert.

"Where you off to?" Reece asked.

"The little cowboy's room," I deadpanned and he laughed, but at the last second, I shot a quick glance Ruth's way. I didn't miss the way her eyes flared at my look, and I moseyed over to the bathrooms, taking my time.

When I heard footsteps behind me as I got to the dark alcove where the restrooms were located, I grinned. Especially when I felt small, feminine hands slip into the back pockets of my Wranglers. "Where you headed, cowboy?"

I spun and there Ruth was, reading my mind just like I hoped she would. I opened the door to one of the two restrooms and slammed it shut behind us. Ruth was right there with me, flicking the lock at the same time the motion-sensor lights flickered the lights on.

Her hands were on the lapels of my suitcoat and she was dragging me toward the narrow counter. "God, I've been dying to get my hands on you all day," she whispered hungrily, and naturally, my cock jerked all the way to attention at hearing her throaty admission.

She hopped up on the counter, tugging me between her legs and wrapping them around my waist as her dress bunched up. God, I loved how perfect that felt. How natural. How the entire day felt like it had been leading to this moment.

I leaned in to kiss her, but she leaned back even as she linked her arms around my neck, a sly smile on her face. "God, you have no idea how much I want to kiss you and then fuck your brains out. But we haven't had a chance to talk all day. How are you? I saw you and Reece coming in with the horses." She withdrew her arms but only so she could run her fingers through the hair at the sides of my head, her nails digging into my scalp. "Did you guys have a good talk?"

I swallowed hard and leaned my weight slightly into her. I'd never really experienced this. The feminine softness of someone touching me like this, wanting to hear about my day or know how I was. Maybe it was the wine addling my head, but suddenly this—*Ruth*—she was all I wanted.

All I'd ever wanted, if I was honest. I leaned my head to the side, so that my cheek was in her palm, my eyes closed. Fuck, but her hands were soft. She grew up doing work as hard as I did every day but her hands were still somehow soft. And they smelled good, like she used some sort of flowery lotion. It made my cock even stiffer, and positioned between her legs like I was, one probe of my hips had me nestling into her heated sex, only my jeans and the skirt of her dress separating me from conquest.

But for once in my life I was content right here, lingering in the before. Only with this woman who had put some sort of hex on me.

I turned my head even further and kissed her palm, then began trailing kisses up her arm. "Talk later?" I asked, my voice full in a way

I couldn't explain. I wasn't sure I could manage talking right now. I was feeling too much. I needed to let the feelings out—to fuck them out. To satiate all of this—this *whatever* it was that was full in my chest.

She smiled and nodded and leaned down, her hands sliding back around my neck, her fingers burying in the slightly longish hair there. I needed a haircut. But then I closed my eyes. Or maybe not, because fuck, I loved the way that felt, her fingernails scraping against my scalp like that as she worked her fingers through my thick hair.

I never let women touch me. But Ruth's touch in this moment, it was electrifying even as it felt dangerous.

And then our lips met. Fuuuuuuuuuuuuck, her lips were soft. And her tongue flicked out as we kissed. She briefly suckled the middle of my upper lip, her tongue working the nerves inside.

I grunted and grabbed her body, jerking her to me tighter. The little vixen had discovered that spot somewhere along the line and knew that right there on my inner upper lip was somehow like a nerve attached straight to my dick.

All of a sudden, I was done with gentle and the strange emotion caught in my chest. My cock wanted inside her sweet little—

Apparently, she was thinking along the same lines, 'cause she flipped up her dress all the way and my mouth went dry. She wasn't wearing any underwear. Fuck. Fuck, she hadn't been wearing any underwear this whole time.

My eyes flew up to her, where she was grinning saucily back at me. "I hoped we'd find some time together tonight."

My hands couldn't drop to my belt fast enough. I didn't bother with niceties. I unbuckled, unbuttoned, unzipped, pulled myself out and then shoved inside her waiting wetness.

We both groaned as I finally slid inside.

Again her arms came around me, clutching me to her, and again, I allowed it.

I hadn't felt a woman's arms around me since... since...

But no, I wouldn't think about that. I breathed in the scent of Ruth, her lotion, her shampoo, her skin, trying to ground myself.

I was here, with Ruth, in this bathroom. My jaw flexed.

Here. Now. I was here. Not there.

Not there.

Still, my chest constricted until I peeled Ruth's arms from around me and pinned them behind her back.

She arched her chest out toward me and spread her legs even wider. "Oh God, yes. Jeremiah, you feel so good."

And just like that, one hand holding both of her wrists tightly, I was back. I opened my eyes and looked down on Ruth so gorgeously splayed out below me on the counter. Her cheeks were splotchy and red with her building pleasure, her lips ruby red.

I huffed out like a bull as I pulled out of her and then shoved roughly back in. Her eyes rolled back as my cock filled her full, so full because goddamn, she was a tight fit.

A knock came at the door behind us. Ruth's alarmed eyes shot to me.

"Occupied," I called out roughly as I dropped the hand not holding her arms to her clit.

Fuck, I loved how wet she got for me. My finger was immediately covered in her juices as I slid my thumb around her clit, rubbing up and down her slit to where my cock was buried inside her. She shuddered underneath my touch.

Fuck, watching her writhe there beneath me made my balls tighten. I massaged her clit while I continued to fuck her. The knocking didn't come again. There were two bathrooms after all, and I wasn't going to be hurried when fucking this gorgeous creature. Never.

In fact, though I loved this angle, I wanted her to watch what I was doing. I wanted her to look in her own face as I fucked her. I wanted to see her face as she watched herself.

But first I'd get her off here. I knew my baby always had more than one in her.

So I pulled out and leaned over, putting my mouth on her dripping cunt.

I'd finally let go of her wrists, a good thing because she slapped a hand over her mouth to quiet the breathy squeals that started up the second I began tonguing her clit.

Fuck, there was nothing sweeter than burying myself chin deep in the right woman. I loved Ruth's pussy. Hers was by far my favorite. With her legs opened wide to me like this, she was like a fully blossomed flower, the lips of her vulva full and flushed with life. When I massaged them with my fingers up and down to her hole and then notched my chin fully inside her slit and latched my mouth onto that little bud of hers—

She just absolutely lost her shit, and it was the most beautiful fucking thing I'd ever witnessed.

Her legs shook. Her torso shuddered. Her little squeals escaped no matter the hand secured over her mouth.

I gave her so much pleasure in that moment, I could feel her world rocking. When her orgasm finally subsided and I stood up, wiping my mouth on my sleeve, she looked at me with pupils blown, slack against the counter, and I took pity on her.

"Should I carry you back to your chair, beautiful?"

But her eyes zeroed in on my hard cock and she shook her head. She only gave me one word: "More."

I grinned at her as I reached for her waist and lifted her off the counter. She was a curvy, lush woman, but still weighed nothing to a guy who tossed around giant hay bales for a living. I lifted her and spun her around so that she was facing the mirror. Together we looked at her flushed cheeks and smeared eye makeup. Her eyes always watered when she had one of those huge, body-rocking orgasms. I grinned at her over her head.

"Brace your arms on the counter, baby," I whispered in her ear as I flipped her skirt back up and rubbed a hand over her soft, sweet little bare ass. I kept going, sliding my hand down between her legs until she let out a needy little whine and bent over, widening her stance so I had better access.

"That's my girl," I cooed in her ear. "Now watch yourself in the mirror as I fuck you. I want to see you watch yourself as I make you come."

Her eyes did the fluttery roll thing as I nudged at her entrance with my cock. I helped feed myself into her slick cunt with my hand and then I pushed in.

She let out a breathy little moan. Goddamn. Every time. Would it ever get old, hearing that noise? I couldn't imagine it ever could.

This was Ruth. Ruth, who'd driven me crazy, never letting a single point go without arguing the hell out of it. But seeing her submit so sweetly, and clench on my cock as I pushed into her... Fuck, but I felt like a king. I bottomed out inside her, and then a wild impulse hit and I put one hand around her neck.

Her eyes in the mirror lifted briefly to meet mine before dropping back to look at her own face. Or rather, to look at my hand on her neck. At which point she nuzzled her ass out and wiggled it, signaling she was into everything I had for her.

A fresh rush of blood hit my cock as I lightly squeezed her dainty little throat and felt her swallow.

What the fuck was this woman doing to me?

I didn't know, but I also didn't take my eyes off her as I fucked her slow and kept a careful pressure on her neck.

She gave me such trust, so completely, so effortlessly.

And I didn't take it easy on her.

With the hand not at her throat I reached between the counter to massage her clit. She was more swollen than I'd ever felt her.

I barely touched her before she was thrashing, pushing forward against my hand at her throat as if looking for even more constriction.

I gave it to her.

And right as I was about to spill into her, unable to handle the erotic scene a moment longer, I released her neck and we both came, her pussy clenching so hard around me I thought my goddamn spine was going to be sucked out through my dick because holy fucking Christ!!

Afterward, we were both bent forward over the counter, me still impaling her, cum leaking out down her leg, and my hand still at her throat, though limp now. I massaged her throat gently and placed kisses at the nape of her neck.

She was so goddamned beautiful, so fucking perfect.

I dropped my hand down to her breast, the other still lost in the wetness of her pussy and I clutched her to myself.

I didn't want to let her go. Didn't want the moment to end. In this post-sex euphoria of what felt like the hardest, most complete orgasm I'd ever experienced, I couldn't let her go.

She was still trembling underneath me and didn't struggle to get away.

So I kept holding her, occasionally swirling my fingers in her pussy and making her body jump and twitch with aftershocks.

It was only another hard knocking at the door that finally broke the spell and had me lifting to stand upright.

I bowed my head into Ruth's back a moment as I finally pulled out of her delicious body, hating that it was over already and we had to separate. I'd never experienced this with a woman. Usually when it was done, I was the one looking for the exit as quickly as I could. But with this damn woman, I just wanted to stay in the moment, I didn't want to let go of her body, or for her body to let go of mine.

The door handle rattled and I turned my head to call out roughly, "Occupied."

Ruth finally roused beneath me, standing up as well and reaching for the paper towel dispenser. No doubt to clean me off her, dripping down her legs. I don't know why the thought had my half-stiff cock jerking. It was a caveman's response, the thought of my cum on her skin arousing me.

I leaned forward just as she finished gathering a wad of towels, and bit the back of her neck, not hard, just enough so that I could taste her skin and feel her shudder beneath me.

She groaned low and then turned in my arms. I took her mouth voraciously. She kissed me just as hungrily back, her arms coming around my neck. For once, I allowed it. I was too hungry to taste her. To feel her kissing me just as hungrily back.

How could we still be this crazy for each other *after* fucking? I grabbed her hair and pulled, ruining the updo just like I'd ruined the rest of her makeup as I tugged her face back from mine. And goddammit, I loved the way her wide, lust-filled eyes came to mine.

"Don't do it," I said, the words spilling out of my mouth on impulse. "You don't belong behind a desk, stuck in a lab somewhere decoding intake data or whatever the fuck you said you'd be doing. You belong on the land. Doing what you love."

She blinked rapidly, her soft body suddenly stiffening. "What are you saying? It's my job. I have to have a job—"

I shook my head and the words just shot out of my mouth. "I'm saying be old-fashioned with me. I'm saying marry me and run this ranch with me and maybe the horse program if you're interested in that too."

She choked and then sputtered, her eyes as wide as saucers. "W-what? Is this a business proposition or did you just— Did you just propose to me?"

I groaned and bent my forehead to hers. "It's coming out wrong, huh? I just, I don't think it's wrong to want to be part of a world where loving a woman means loving her through and through. I want it all. Could I have ever imagined a woman who loves the same kinda life I love, is smart as a fuckin' whip, smarter than *me* sometimes—which, being the ass that I am, grates for about five seconds before it just turns me the fuck on? No. No, I never even fucking dreamed there was a woman out there like you." Saying it all out loud, I realized how true it was. And how much I wanted her. As my wife. In my bed. Always.

"Oh." She blinked hard, still looking shell-shocked.

I grabbed her by the back of my neck and pulled her in close. Sure, what I was doing was fucking nuts, but people fell in love fast all the time, just look at my brother and Charlie.

"What I'm trying to say is, this is what love is. The oh-shit-this-one-actually-checks-all-the-boxes part and the I-want-to-wring-her-neck-or-fuck-each-others-brains-out-nonstop part together. That's love."

She blinked up at me. "A-Are you sure?"

I grinned at her, an elated feeling lighting up my chest. "I don't fucking know. But I've never felt anything like this before. You're all I can think about. I used to get so mad at my brother for falling in love with some woman or other, left and right, I never understood why he got so moon-eyed—"

"No." She shook her head goofily back at me and interlaced our fingers. "Me too. I was always so cautious in relationships. Never opening up or letting myself be vulnerable." She shook her head in a grimace and made a slice across her neck with her finger. "Never."

"So this," I said, my voice deepening as I stepped closer, our chests touching, "I'm the only one you're letting this close."

"This is crazy," she giggled, running her hands through my hair. "Are we really doing this?"

I pulled away from her far enough so that I could go down on one knee. She still had the wad of paper towels in her hand and she was disheveled as all hell. She'd never looked more radiant. And I wanted to do this right, even if I didn't have a ring yet. I'd fix that as soon as I could.

"Ruth Harshbarger, will you marry me?"

"Yes!" she whispered in voice so full of joy, I knew she felt the elation too. And then she pulled me to my feet and cemented her body to mine as we locked lips.

17

Ruth

It was Charlie's wedding day, the day all the planning had been leading up to, but I'd barely slept a wink last night.

Jeremiah had proposed.

Proposed!

I was engaged.

I mean, holy crap. We'd agreed not to tell anyone. Neither of us wanted to take away from Reece and Charlie's special day.

But about every three seconds, I'd have a little internal giddy freak out. Jeremiah wanted to marry me! We were going to get married. Jeremiah loved me!

I smiled to myself as I finished tying a bow with a little bit of tulle around the last of the chairs. Everything was almost ready for the ceremony. We'd been running around nonstop all day. I'd barely gotten to say two words to Jeremiah other than him stealing me away for a brief two-minute make out session when I ran inside the bunkhouse to grab a protein bar.

Last night we hadn't gotten any more time with each other after

I'd finally put myself back together and made what I could of my smudged makeup. Luckily, when we finally stumbled out of the bathroom, the party was breaking up. Jeremiah waited until I got into my Lyft before he got into the van they'd rented to take everyone else back to the ranch—Matt had volunteered to be the DD for the night.

My grin was big as I looked out on the finished product of the day's hard work. Part of me was shocked it had all come together. Yeah, I'd been on the phone for half the day, and while the catering van from the Salt Lick had been on time, the tables for all the food to go *on* had naturally shown up late.

But all the guys had pitched in, even Xavier's eldest boy, and everything was finally ready. The yard was absolutely *dripping* with flowers. The florists had really gone above and beyond. A stunning installation of white orchids and other flowers covered the archway at the end of the aisle the bride would be arriving through. Flower bedecked trellises were set up alongside the serving tables as well. They'd turned the yard into a mini-Eden. It was magical.

Just in time too, because the guests would start arriving any minute.

It was a hot day but that was to be expected, and under the shade of the large oak, where we'd staged the chairs and ceremony platform, with a breeze, it was almost pleasant as far as Texas was concerned. Especially as the sun started to drop. If the timing went right, Reece and Charlie would be saying their vows right at sunset.

I sighed happily. The pictures would be spectacular. Which reminded me—

But when I looked around, panic only briefly spiking— I breathed out in relief. There was the photographer, taking some preliminary shots, doing their thing.

Everything really was going off without a hitch.

I laughed to myself.

Wow, I was just so used to catastrophe after catastrophe, I almost didn't know what to do when things went well.

My hands lifted to my heated cheeks. Okay, the only thing left was for me to go change. I was a sweaty mess from running around all day. And I should go check in on Charlie and make sure she was on schedule. She should be finishing up hair and makeup. And it'd be good to make sure Momzilla wasn't driving her too nuts.

I headed back around the big house toward the front entrance, a huge grin still on my face. God, my face hurt from smiling so much.

Because once again my thoughts were circling back to my secret joy.

Jeremiah *loved* me. After all my months of crushing on him, imagining what it would be like to...he not only liked me back, he *loved* me.

Pleasure and happiness flushed through me. I'd never been happier in my whole *life*.

Then a tiny voice chimed in, one I'd been trying to ignore all day, and I frowned: He didn't actually say *I love you*.

I shook it off. He'd said, "this is what love is," and that was essentially the same thing. I was being nit-picky and stupid to want him to say it in a particular way, like it was some magic formula.

I pulled open the front door just in time to hear Charlie's voice sounding tense. "It's fine, Mom. This is the way I like it."

"But if you just put in these extensions I brought, you could have a proper updo. There's still time to change it. Think of the pictures, darling. You don't want to look like a boy in your own wedding pictures. Or worse, a lesbian!"

"Mother!" Charlie sounded officially pissed now, and I didn't blame her.

I hurried through the foyer and into the bedroom. "Hiiiii," I sing-songed. Charlie was seated in front of a makeshift vanity the makeup and hair artist had set up. She was standing off to the side looking uncomfortable as Charlie glared up at her mother. Mrs. Winston stood haughtily beside her, long hair extensions in her hands. If I hadn't known what they were, I would've thought she was holding some kind of animal.

I averted my eyes back to Charlie and I clapped my hands. "Babe, you look amazing!" And she did. Her pixie hair cut was adorable and her makeup perfect. Understated but perfectly done. Her eyes were highlighted and looked huge and Bambi-ish, with long dark lashes. Her hair had been slightly styled with little flowers pinned here and there.

She looked like an elven princess, an effect I knew would only be enhanced once she got into the beautiful, flowy lace dress she'd picked out.

"You're perfect," I whispered, just for her.

Her eyes met mine and she smiled. "Yeah?"

"Yeah," I nodded.

"That's what I've been telling her," Olivia said from where she'd been sitting on the bed. She was dressed in a simple sundress, lovely as always.

"Which is good." I looked down at my watch. "Because guests are going to start arriving any minute and we're T minus forty until the ceremony starts. No more changes to hair or makeup. It's time to get into the dress!"

Charlie grinned at me, then up at her mom. "See, no more time to change things."

"Here," I pulled my phone out of my pocket. "I'll text the photographer so they can come in and get pics of you putting on the dress."

Everyone nodded and I shot off a quick text. I'd chosen a female photographer specifically for this purpose.

As I finished sending the text, I saw an unread message from Jeremiah.

THINKING OF YOU, GORGEOUS. YOU BEEN DRIVING ME MAD IN THOSE SEXY LEGGINGS ALL DAY. CAN A FIANCÉ STEAL A MINUTE WITH HIS WOMAN ANYTIME TODAY?

I grinned, but then remembered I had to get dressed myself. I shook my head happily as I shot off a quick text back. PATIENCE IS A VIRTUE. I'M GETTING CHANGED WITH CHARLIE. SEE YOU WHEN WE WALK DOWN THE AISLE.

I felt such a surging thrill as I sent the text. Because as I'd set up everything today, all I could think was that one day soon, I'd be doing all this for myself.

Could life really work out like this? One day everything changes and suddenly you get everything you ever wanted and all your dreams come true?

I would get to stay on the land I always loved, the land my family had worked for generations. Even if I didn't own it anymore, what did that matter? Could we ever really *own* land anyway? I'd get to live here, and with the man of my dreams.

It was almost too much. My face was going to hurt from smiling—my cheeks were already sore. Still, I couldn't stop as I slipped into the bathroom and gave myself a quick sponge bath under my arms to get refreshed. I yanked the deodorant out of my large purse and reapplied it, then hastily put on some makeup.

I rejoined Charlie in just my bra and underwear since my dress was on a hanger in her room. She was just stepping into her gown. Her mother was helping her with the buttons from behind, and the photographer was there, the shutter on her camera snapping away.

I slid behind them and hurried to put on my own dress, a peachy ModCloth dress that Olivia found for me. It was tight on the bodice and then got all floofy at the bottom, like a retro fifties dress. It did look fabulous on me—I was shocked at how feminine I felt when I put it on after it came in the mail. For a girl who was used to wranglers, being covered in mud, and smelling more like cows than perfume, feeling so girly was a nice change.

When I looked up, the photo op was finished, or had at least stopped, because Mrs. Winston was frowning down at the buttons. "I've been telling you to restrict calories all week, but did you listen to me? No, of course you didn't. And now we can barely button your gown." She shook her head, her tight lips pursed.

"Here, why don't I try?" Olivia took over working on the long line of buttons up the back of the dress as Charlie's alarmed eyes flashed toward me.

The pregnancy really wasn't showing but I guessed looking at her now, I could see some changes. Her breasts were more full and overall she just looked really healthy—far better than the starved-looking waif who'd first showed up on the ranch eight months ago.

"Reece is going to be grouchy about all these buttons tonight," Olivia joked, breaking the tension.

Mrs. Winston made a disgruntled noise like such things were not to be talked about in civilized company, but Charlie just giggled and glanced over her shoulder. "Right?"

And I grinned harder thinking about how I'd just reminded my own Walker twin that patience was a virtue.

I went over to Charlie and clapped my hands excitedly. "You're perfect. Reece is gonna shit himself when he sees you." I ignored Mrs. Winston's noise of dismay at my curse. I was done tiptoeing around her. I'd done my job. This was Charlie's moment now, and she was one of my best friends.

I threw my arms around her, careful not to smudge any of her makeup or to disturb her hair. "I'm so proud and happy for you," I whispered to her. "You deserve happiness more than anyone else I know."

When I pulled back, her eyes were shining and she swatted at me before fanning her face. "Don't make me cry, bitch. We just finished my makeup."

"Oh, don't worry," the makeup artist said from the corner where she was packing up. "I do weddings all the time. That's why I put so much fixative on at the end. That makeup is waterproof and tear-proof. So make sure to use the makeup remover I gave you at the end of the night to get it all off."

Charlie laughed and nodded gratefully, gently dabbing at her eyes with a cloth Olivia magically produced.

The photographer jumped in and snapped several more pics of all of us.

With Charlie finally buttoned into her dress, there was only a little bit more waiting until it was time.

"Let me go make sure all the groomsmen are where they ought to be," I said and Charlie nodded.

But when I stepped outside, Jeremiah was there, and he had Mike with him. Mike and Reece had gotten close over the past six months, far closer than he ever had with Buck, who either stuck to himself, or was out with various girlfriends, or who knew where the rest of the time he wasn't working. He'd been invited to the wedding but I hadn't seen him around all day. The other good friends Reece had back at Xavier and Mel's couldn't get away since they'd had to stay back at Mel's ranch to run it.

Reece had sworn he didn't mind who all was there, as long as he was walking away with Charlie at the end of the day.

"Ready?" Jeremiah asked me, and just seeing him, being near him, once again had that stupid grin busting out across my face. I nodded, not quite trusting my voice. Then I cleared my throat because, Jesus, I wasn't some stupid teenager.

Though he made me feel like one when he leaned in and whispered in my ear, "Goddamn, you're beautiful. I want to rip that dress right off you. It's gonna be torture making it through this ceremony."

I pulled away, my face flushed, and I was glad that Mike was absorbed in his phone. I mean, God, the intimate way Jeremiah had just pulled me into him, if Mike glanced this way, he'd be an idiot not to guess that we were—

But then again, if we were going to get married, we'd be telling everybody soon enough. It would only be a secret a little longer. We just needed to make it through the day. Another giddy thrill ran through me and I allowed my hand to drop to Jeremiah's for a quick squeeze before letting go.

"Let me just go get Olivia. Poor Charlie. She's had nerves all day. Her mom's not helping, naturally. And oh my God," I leaned into Jeremiah confidentially, "I swear I almost had a heart attack when her mom was buttoning up the dress and started in on Charlie about gaining weight! We've managed to keep the baby secret this whole time and then right before the wedding she almost—"

"Baby?" Jeremiah jerked away from me and I realized my huge faux pas a second too late.

I clapped a hand across my mouth. It was just a slip of the tongue. I'd gotten used to him being my confidante. I'd totally forgotten that Reece wanted this secret kept from him too.

"Shhhh. Hush," I waved my hands frantically at him, glancing again over at Mike, who had looked our way and then quickly back down at his screen.

I stepped in close to Jeremiah and whispered. "Shh, don't say anything. I forgot. They wanted to keep it a secret from everyone till after the wedding."

But Jeremiah was looking anything but calm. He grabbed me by the elbow and dragged me several feet away from Mike. "Are you seriously telling me that my little brother knocked Charlotte up? This is a fucking shotgun wedding?" He shook his head and swore. "I shoulda known this was too good to be true. Reece didn't change at all. He's still just an irresponsible little—"

"Uh, excuse me?" I made a disbelieving noise. "Your brother is not irresponsible. He's great."

Jeremiah looked at me like I was a naïve idiot. "Oh, come on. You think this means true love?" He scoffed. "We all thought it was weird, them getting married so fast. It's the oldest story in the book. Our dad married our mom for the same reason. And he was gone three months after we were born, so don't tell me about how *great* my brother is. He's just repeating history."

I took a step back from him.

Mainly so I wouldn't slap him.

"How can you say that? You know him better than anyone."

He looked at me and his eyes were hard. "Exactly."

I just shook my head, my heart hurting for Reece. To have grown up with someone so judgmental at your side, always expecting you to fuck up and then saying *I told you so* every time you made a mistake...

And this was the man I was planning to make a life with?

The internal question hit me like a kick in the guts. It was like everything was crashing down in waves. I tried to push away the thought but Jeremiah stood there in front of me looking so angry, stubborn, and intractable.

Then, behind us, Olivia opened the door. "Oh good, everyone's here," she said, her face bright. "It's time, isn't it, Ruth? Charlie's getting antsy in here."

Oh God. Charlie. It was Charlie's day. Charlie and Reece. They were getting married, come hell or high water.

Or a stubborn, annoying twin brother who would *not*, I repeat *not*, interfere with this wedding going forward.

I forced a smile for Olivia. "Just give us one more minute."

Thankfully, Jeremiah stayed quiet until the door shut again. Then I grabbed his lapels and jerked him close and spoke about two inches away from his face to make sure he got the message.

"Listen here. You are *not* going to fuck up this day for your brother. I don't care *what* you think about it. Reece loves Charlotte and she loves him back. They are going to have a perfect wedding day and you aren't going to say one goddamned *word* about this. Do you get me?"

He stared at me stone-faced and I jerked his lapels again. "Nod if you get me."

He shrugged me off but nodded, standing stiffly upright like a rod had been shoved up his ass.

I let go of him and let out a long rush of breath. "Fine. Let's get through this."

All of the day's joy turned to dread as I opened the door to retrieve Olivia, Charlie, and her parents.

"It's time!" I said as brightly as I could. Charlie frowned at me, always too perceptive for her own good. But thankfully, she was distracted by hearing the wedding music change. We'd carefully picked out the music, and she knew it was the song before the wedding march began.

I tried to enjoy her eyes lighting up, but my stomach was still sour with Jeremiah's accusations. Reece wasn't like their father. He would never leave this beautiful woman or their child in the dust. He *had* grown up, and if his own brother couldn't see that, all the more tragedy when everyone else could.

"Daddy?" Charlotte looked toward her father, who must have joined her while I was outside. He looked tall and refined in a tux as he stood to take her arm. Her mother wasn't anywhere to be seen and I assumed she'd gone to take her seat in the front row.

The vulnerability in Charlie's eyes as she looked toward her dad made me forget Jeremiah and everything else.

This *was* her day, and in spite of her terrible mother I was still so glad we could give her this. I was happy her parents were here for this and that they were finally supporting her. God knew we couldn't choose our family. Sometimes showing up was enough.

When I next smiled at Charlie, it was genuine. "Come on," I motioned toward them. "It's time."

I prayed that Jeremiah had gotten his shit together by the time we stepped outside. I hurried in front of Charlie and her dad to push out the door first, just in case I needed to shoot him the evil eye to get him in line. But when I stepped outside, Jeremiah was standing in line beside Mike, a pleasant enough expression on his face, even if he was standing a little stiffer than usual.

Good enough.

"All right," I said, infusing my voice with a cheer I didn't necessarily feel anymore, "it's time, everybody! Places, places!"

Olivia came out of the house last and scurried ahead of me to take Mike's arm while I lined up behind her and took Jeremiah's. Charlie and her dad were behind us. It was a small wedding party, sure, but all Reece and Charlie needed.

We'd run through this all last night, but my stomach was aflutter with butterflies. As we all walked around the corner of the house right as the music changed to Pachelbel's Canon, I yanked Jeremiah down by his arm so I could hiss at him, "Promise you won't make a scene."

He jerked back and glared down at me. "I know how to behave myself."

I breathed out in relief, but he just shook his head like he had a bad taste in his mouth. Whatever. We had a wedding to pull off. I couldn't care about his *feelings* right now. Especially when his feelings were so stupid.

I tried to push down my anger at him for even reacting the way he had, but took another deep breath as we all gathered behind the group of tall bushes the florists had brought in to block the seated crowd's view of us. Who did he think he was, anyway, Mr. High and Mighty?

Shake it off, shake it off, I told myself as Olivia and Matt started their arm-in-arm march down the aisle in front of us. And fucking *smile*.

I flashed my teeth and hoped it looked cheerful and not like a grimace as Jeremiah and I stepped out on cue once Olivia and Matt were halfway down the aisle.

The music chimed out all around from strategically placed speakers. The crowd was full, almost every seat taken. No one in town was gonna miss a chance at food and a spectacle like this, even if both Reece and Charlie were relative newcomers. The Harshbarger Ranch was an institution around here, and everyone had been curious to see the new build after the twister took the old house off.

I was glad. It gave a festive cheer to the event. I knew every face in the crowd and most of them I'd at least introduced Charlie to. Hopefully, even more friendships could come out of this, cementing her and Reece's place in the community.

And looking ahead at Reece waiting beside the huge Xavier, he couldn't have looked more different from his twin. He was grinning goofily, leaning dramatically to the side like he was trying to peek around me and Jeremiah to get even a glimpse of his bride. Reece was sweet and nonjudgmental and playful and—

Everything his brother was not.

I clutched Jeremiah's arm tighter as we reached the front of the aisle. I was hesitant to let go of him and go stand on the opposite side of the altar. I knew he'd promised he wouldn't make waves, but I seriously swore that I would strangle the bastard if he ruined this for my friends.

But when he finally unpeeled my arm from his, still with a glare, he at least stayed silent when he went to stand beside his brother. It took everything I could not to bite my nails as they stood side by side, features identical and yet still, never more opposite.

Jeremiah stood stiff as a soldier while Reece was grinning so big I thought his face might split in half when Charlotte finally appeared at the top of the aisle and the music changed to the wedding march. Not to mention the tears I saw cresting in his eyes. He didn't wipe them away, either. No. He just stared in awe at his wife-to-be as her father brought her down the aisle to him.

When her dad lifted the veil and he saw her face to face, the tears fell and still he didn't seem to care. He pulled Charlie close and dropped his forehead to hers as he whispered something to her I couldn't hear. But I could read her corresponding smile and read the body language as she sank into him, the lines between them disappearing for a moment before she pulled back, only their hands linked.

They both grinned like fools throughout the entire ceremony, repeating after Xavier with sometimes wobbly voices. Charlie was openly crying by the end, but the makeup artist was true to her word, her makeup didn't smudge one bit.

Jeremiah kept up his stupid stoic stance the whole time but I ignored him and lost myself in the romantic moment of my best friends uniting in love.

When Xavier finally announced, "You may kiss the bride," the crowd got to its feet and cheered as Reece dipped Charlie and kissed her deep. And uh… for a good long while. Whistles and laughter came from the crowd until, long moments later, he lifted her back upright and released her. They were both grinning and laughing, including Xavier, who only looked slightly more terrifying when he laughed.

"I now pronounce you husband and wife!" Xavier declared.

I felt a wave of relief wash through my body. Holy shit. We'd actually done it. They were married now, with no major hiccups. I laughed along with everyone else as the couple walked back down the aisle. Everyone opened the little bags of birdseed they'd been given and they tossed it on the newlyweds as they passed.

And then it was on to the reception, just in the field off to the side. We'd put up a big tent for the reception (in case of rain) yesterday along with tables. All the guests helped move the chairs from the ceremony space into the tent around the tables while Reece and Charlie took a moment to refresh themselves inside.

"Yes, over there," I guided some guests where to go. "Yep. Barbeque from the Salt Lick is the main course but there are vegetarian options too."

They thanked me and then moved past, chairs in tow.

And then Jeremiah was in front of me, towering and blocking the Texas sun. "You. We need to talk."

I pursed my lips. "Can it wait? I'm kind of busy here."

Jeremiah looked around. "Everyone's figuring it out. Then they stand around and eat. It's self-explanatory. Come on." And he took my elbow and started dragging me to the side of the house nearest the bunkhouse, where there weren't any guests. "We need to talk."

"Fine," I said, jerking out of his hold. "There's no need to manhandle me."

As soon as we were around the corner and away from prying eyes, he started spitting accusations at me. "How could you not tell me my brother had knocked Charlie up? I fucking *proposed* to you but you were keeping something this huge a secret from me? In what world is that fucking okay?"

I blinked at him and crossed my arms over my chest. "Excuse me? You wanna maybe rethink your tone? I'm not your brother's keeper, and by the way, neither are you. Charlie's my best friend and she asked me to keep a secret."

"And I was going to be your *husband*!" he all but shouted.

I sucked in a breath and only managed to eke out a single word. "Was?" followed by a choked out, "Past tense?"

He threw a hand out. "Oh, come on. You really think we'd work? I was basing that on some romantic nonsense thinking my brother had finally—" He shook his head hard, and it was like with every second he was becoming more remote. "But he hasn't changed, not really, because people don't. No one ever changes. Shit will always fall apart and I have to be the smart brother who doesn't let himself get caught up in it. I can't get distracted or— Or whatever fantasy land we were living in."

I stepped back. He might as well have punched me in the face. He didn't want me. That was all he was really saying. He was using a bunch of other words, but I heard what it boiled down to. He didn't want me.

Fucking fine, that was a familiar enough feeling in my life.

"Fuck you!" I lunged forward and shoved his chest. "Fuck *you* for pretending to—"

"To what? Have all my shit together?" He held out his hands and I frowned, because that hadn't been what I was about to say. "I don't!"

"Oh, that's more than obvious. It's clear you're no more mature than all those little pricks I fucked in high school."

He caught my arm and looked at me hard. "Careful."

I just shook my head, giving him a venomous smile back. "Oh wow, look at the big man. You wanna knock me around some now, huh?"

"What? Jesus." He let go of me and backed away. "Fuck. You don't know me at all, do you?"

And tears burst from my eyes because I did know him, dammit, and it was the only reason I'd let him in so deep. But none of it mattered. Because now here he was breaking my heart anyway.

I looked up at him through my tears. "Why are we fighting again?" When what I really wanted to ask was, "Why are you doing this to me?" and to beg him to take the last five minutes back.

And I wanted him to laugh at me and say he didn't know why we were fighting and then pull me into his arms and run his fingers through my hair. I wanted him to say everything would be all right, or we'd figure it out tomorrow after everything cooled down.

But he didn't say any of those things.

He looked at me, his brown eyes full of sorrow, and said, "I think it's because we were never meant to be. Two people who drive each other this mad—"

I shook my head, scoffing. "That's what you said love was. The I-want-to-wring-his-neck-and-also-fuck-his-brains-out-at-the-same-time. Remember? And being the only ones who checked all each other's boxes?"

Again he held his arms up, looking at a loss for words. "Maybe that was just—"

A woman could only handle so much. "A what?" I asked. "An idiot mistaking lust for love?"

He stood there looking miserable in front of me.

I breathed in. And I breathed out. My guts were twisting inside and embarrassment flamed my cheeks red hot. But right behind that was icy anger.

I looked down at the ground, collected myself, and then marched the few feet I'd put between us to where Jeremiah stood. And, in a single fluid motion, I slapped the bastard hard across the cheek.

"That," I said into the stinging silence that followed, my face only inches from his, "is because you're a liar, Jeremiah Walker, and a coward." I pointed my finger in his face. "Because I know you felt it too. And it was the real fucking thing."

And then I turned on my booted heel and walked my ass away from him and out of his *life*.

∼

OR I WOULD HAVE, anyway, if there was any justice in the universe and I wasn't still obligated to go spend the next few hours at his twin brother's wedding reception.

Having your heart ripped out, shredded into pieces, and then stomped on—and then having to smile and pretend like everything was wonderful and you were just *so* happy for your friends, one of whom just happened to look like the man who'd smashed your heart into bits—not my idea of a great day.

But today wasn't about me, so I grinned and bore it anyway.

At least Jeremiah stayed away from me. But as I busied myself pretending to fuss over catering and helping the servers keep everything restocked—the tables and champagne flutes, I was steadily bleeding out from the inside.

Which was stupid. We'd only been engaged for a single night—not even twenty-four hours. And he'd been drunk last night—or at least a little wine and sex hazed. I should have known he wouldn't mean it in the morning. Stupid. I'd been so *stupid* to let myself believe, for even a second, that—

"Hey, are you ready, they're about to cut the cake—" Olivia said as she caught me in an unguarded moment hiding behind the catering truck. "Whoa. Are you okay? Did something happen?"

I tried to wave my hand and blink back stupid tears. "It's nothing. I'm fine."

She crossed her arms and blocked my path. "Uh uh. I've known you since second grade, Ruth. I know when you're lying. What happened? Did someone say something nasty about your dad? Who was it? I'll punch them."

I laughed through my tears and swiped at my eyes, then lurched forward and hugged my friend. "God, you're the best. I'm going to miss you so much."

She stiffened slightly in my arms and pulled back. "Miss me? Where the hell are you going?"

I breathed out and swiped again at my face. Shit. My makeup was going to smear if I didn't stop it soon. I didn't have Charlie's mega-mascara on, just the cheap grocery store kind.

I looked my longtime friend in the eye and breathed out hard. God, it hurt, the brief future I'd allowed myself to envision along with Jeremiah's faux-prosal. But it was gone and now I was back to reality.

"I've taken a job up near Fort Worth. I leave in a few weeks. I didn't want the news to overshadow the wedding so I haven't told anyone."

Olivia's mouth dropped open in shock. "Not even me?" She sounded hurt and now that we were here, I could see what a dick move it was.

"I'm so sorry, hon. I think I just didn't want…" I shook my head. "I didn't want to admit I was really going." I looked out at the land I'd so long called home, that I'd fought so hard to hold onto. "Everything's changing." I looked back at her. "But you and me are family and nothing will change that."

Now she was the one with tears in her eyes and she pulled me back in for another hug. "Nothing'll be the same around here without you, bitch," she whispered in my ear. "Whose gonna be my drinking buddy now?"

I laughed. "Well, luckily you've still got Charlie. She's not going anywhere."

But Olivia just shook her head. "It's supposed to be the three of us. And now she's getting married. And having a baby. You're moving onto some awesome career. And I'm still just here. Same as always."

"Don't say that. You're fabulous. And I'll come back and visit all the time. It's only a three-hour trip back. I'll be back so much and crashing on your couch you'll be sick of me."

She looked up at me, her lovely features crumpled. "Promise?"

"Promise."

We both laughed a little and then she said, "Jesus, look at us!" She reached in her purse and produced a compact and packet of tissues. "They're about to cut the cake and we'll look like goth chicks with these black tear tracks in the pictures if we don't clean up!"

We hurriedly swiped at our eyes and then Olivia dabbed fresh concealer under her eyes and then offered it to me. We were nearly presentable if a little puffy eyed by the time we made our way back to the party group all gathered near the cake.

Charlie was glowing as she stood by Reece, who looked like he'd just won the lottery as he stared down at his bride. It hurt, seeing that face with that look of love on it. Not that Jeremiah would ever look that way at anybody. He'd never allow himself that kind of vulnerability. Everything in me wanted to look around and clock where the evil twin brother was, but no, I forced my eyes to stay on the happy couple.

Charlie glanced out at the crowd, briefly making eye contact with Olivia and me before grinning and spinning around so that her back was to us again.

She tossed the colorful bouquet backward over her head and, as if in slow motion, I could see it heading right toward me. It would have been easy to reach out and pluck it from the air. It would hit me straight in the center of the chest if I didn't.

So I stepped backward several steps and Olivia had to dive sideways in a daring last-minute catch before the flowers hit the ground.

Around us, the crowd cheered her, but as Charlie turned around to look at us, I could see her eyes were quizzical when she saw how far away I was standing from where I'd previously been.

I just couldn't, though, not even for my friend. Even such a silly tradition hurt too bad in light of Jeremiah's retracted proposal.

"Now for the cutting of the cake!" I announced, forcing a wide, happy grin over my face as I beamed at the couple as if my heart wasn't being forced through a shredder.

Reece took Charlie's arm as he led her the few feet toward the huge, tiered wedding cake set up on a card table near the tent's northernmost corner. The crowd followed, happy murmurs and the clink of glassware as champagne flutes as people drank deeply.

In fact, the day could not have turned out more perfect. For once, the day was cooler than usual. It was only in the mid-nineties instead of sweltering over the hundred-degree mark. Under the tent it was positively cozy, especially with the mid-afternoon breeze.

Yes, everyone was using the printed wedding bulletins as makeshift fans, but that was just a habit from church.

The caterer had already cut two perfect pieces of cake for Reece and Charlie, so they only had to pick up their individual plates. Reece forked a delicate bite and slid it into Charlie's mouth. She swallowed it quickly, then reached out with her hand to grab Reece's piece, snatched half of it up, and shoved it in his face.

Before she could stop him, he snatched her up and kissed her, smashing the already smushed cake between them.

It would have been a sweet, funny moment.

It really would have.

If only the bride hadn't pulled away in alarm seconds later with a warning hand up and a slightly green looking face. Then she slapped a hand over her mouth, turned, and fled for the edge of the tent. Lucky for her, it wasn't far.

And then everyone who was gathered so closely around had the undue pleasure of hearing Charlie throw up all that she'd managed to get down this morning and afternoon.

Reece immediately rushed to her side, rubbing her back, and handing her a napkin. But overall, he didn't look too surprised or worried. Something I apparently wasn't the only one to notice.

"Charlotte?" a voice rang out. And then suddenly Charlie's mom was pushing through the crowd. "Honey what's— Did you have something bad? Did you eat the beef or the chicken, because I had the chicken and I can't afford—" And then her mother stopped, gasping. "Oh my God, are you pregnant?"

And the anvil dropped.

Charlie could have lied. It would have been easy to shake her head and save her dignity in the moment, in front of the whole town no less.

God, I could have killed Mrs. Winston in that moment. Why did she have to air family laundry in front of this group of relative strangers? She didn't know these people from Adam, but Charlie and Reece *lived here*. And gossip like this traveled faster than a tick on a spooked deer. Everyone would know by sundown.

I expected Charlie to shrink away or try to placate her mom like she had every other time on this trip.

Instead, she surprised the hell out of me. She snatched the napkin out of Reece's hand, wiped her mouth, then walked over to her mother and stood up tall to her.

"I'll have you know that it is my *honor* to announce," she hooked her arm through Reece's and jerked him possessively to her side, "I am *honored* to be having a baby with this man. Maybe we should have been honest from the start. It was definitely one of the reasons that made us choose to get married, but it was far from the only one. I love this man, through and through. Everything he is and everything he will become."

Then she turned back to Reece and clasped her hands like they had back at the diner. "I'm fucking ecstatic to get to partner at your side as you go on the journey, love. It's the honor and pleasure of my life. And I, for one, cannot *wait* to see you as a father. You're going to be amazing at it."

Then she spun back on her mother. "But *you*. We've all been walking around on eggshells ever since you got here, all because I wanted to preserve some kind of relationship with you so my child would have grandparents to know and love. But I should have known that anyone who could stand passively by while their daughter was married to an abusive monster, even when I *told* you, I *begged* you for help—"

Her mother waved a hand to cut her daughter off, the high color in her cheeks evidence enough that she didn't appreciate having the tables turned on her and having *her* dirty laundry aired in front of the public instead. Her mother leaned in and hissed, "You always were an overly dramatic child," Mrs. Winston snapped. "We thought you were just exaggerating for attention. And considering this little display, I can't be sure we were wrong. When you make a *commitment* to a man, you stick to it. But no, the first time you ran into a little adversity, you wanted to quit your marriage. Of course I counseled you the way I did, and I stick by it. Jeffrey was an excellent husband and it's a tragedy we lost him the way we did."

"Leave." Reece said, stepping in front of his wife. "Go. Right now. You're no longer welcome here."

Mrs. Winston tried to look around him at her daughter, her face the picture of offense, but Charlie had turned away from her, burying her face in her husband's back. She glared back up at Reece. "Who are you to speak to me that way? Who are your people? Oh right, you're *nobody*. You're nothing. You think you're so much better than Jeffrey, taking advantage of my daughter when she was vulnerable and chaining her to this dead-end life by planting your bastard in her belly—"

"Mother! That's enough. Reece is right. You're welcome to leave now. I wanted you in our child's life but not if you're going to be like this. I've chosen my family now—real family so that for the first time in my life I understand the meaning of the word. If you ever want to be part of it again, things will have to change. Either way, I need you to leave right now."

Then Charlie turned back to Reece and the way they looked at each other in that moment, it might as well have been as if the hundred and fifty of their closest friends and relatives around them had all disappeared.

Charlie threw her arms around Reece and tucked her face into his chest as he enveloped her in the safest, most secure looking hug in the world. My chest hurt just watching them, especially as they continued ignoring everyone, including Charlie's parents. Reece kept his arm securely tucked around her shoulder as they walked back toward the house.

"The bride needs some rest. Keep celebrating, enjoy the food and open bar and I'll be right back!" Reece called over his shoulder.

Mrs. Winston just huffed and crossed her arms over her chest, her lips thinned in disapproval. "It's a *disgrace*. A bastard conceived out of wedlock. My grandfather must be rolling over in his grave to see what's happened to his bloodline. We were raised better."

If I punched the mother of the bride at her own daughter's wedding, that would be a *bad* thing, right? Especially since I still had one last check for fifteen grand to secure from her.

My hand was still itchy anyway.

No chance though because then she was grabbing her husband's arm and dragging him back around the house. The man hadn't said a single word during the altercation between his wife and daughter. But he hurried along at his wife heels. House-trained for sure, that one. I bet he didn't even pee on the carpet anymore. Lord only knows how Charlie came from those two—one of nature's little miracles.

Not that there was anywhere for them to go—I was their ride back to the airport.

Maybe I could do something crazy for once and actually... enjoy the wedding I'd worked so hard to put together?

Especially since I saw Jeremiah walking in the direction of the house. If he was going to confront his brother about the pregnancy, well, I was full up on drama for today, thank you very much.

People were starting to flow out onto the dance floor as the band really got going. I'd just check one last time with the caterers that we weren't running low on anything and then I'd go catch up with Olivia where I could see her seated across the tent at the open bar.

After the day I'd had, an open bar sounded *juuuust* about right.

But it turned out when I found the caterer, they were freaking out about a second van with the second course getting lost, and by the time we'd helped them navigate to the ranch, it was almost sunset. I was about to start looking for Olivia again when my phone buzzed in my pocket. I'd left it on vibrate ever since the service earlier but kept it close in case of any last-minute catering or supply emergencies.

I pulled it out and looked at the screen. An incoming call was coming from an unfamiliar number, but considering all the people I was wrangling today, that wasn't surprising.

I clicked the green button and raised it to my ear, stepping a little into darkness and closing my other ear with my finger against the loud music in the background. "Hello? This is Ruth."

"Ruth. Buck here. The Winstons wanted to go back to the airport and I couldn't come up with a reason not to. So we're halfway to Austin but I'm stopped at a rest stop off highway 12. Right before it hits 71. You can't miss us. I overheard them saying something about a check they owe you? They're trying to drive and dash, but I'll stall 'em if you hurry. Say the SUV's overheated."

"Shit," I swore, dragging a hand through my hair. I was depending on that money. They'd signed a contract and them turning out to be unhappy with their daughter was no reason to stiff me for all the work I'd done. That wasn't how contracts worked. Plus, yes, most of it was my commission, but three thousand of it was still what I owed on the bar tab, due at the end of the night! They couldn't just—

Infuriated, I snapped into the phone, "Thanks, Buck. Don't let them move a muscle. I'm on my way. Be there in fifteen." My eyes fell on Olivia's sporty little Honda. She wouldn't mind me borrowing it for a good cause. "Or less," I finished, then hung up and started texting Olivia as I jogged toward her car.

As expected, the keys were up in the sun visor. I hopped in and navigated around the makeshift parking lot that had been created out of our front field. I gunned it as soon as I was out of earshot of the wedding and didn't take my foot off the pedal until I neared the 71 switchoff.

It was full dark by the time I got there, but I found the sign for the rest stop. Good God. If the Winstons were pissed earlier, they'd be doubly so essentially being held captive at the side of the road by a roughneck cowboy like Buck.

I was truly surprised at him coming through like this. Usually he was so standoffish, I was a bit shocked for him to have even gotten involved at all. We'd invited everyone who lived on the ranch to the wedding, of course, but everyone else had been part of the wedding party, and it only occurred to me now to wonder if Buck had felt left out. I hadn't seen him anywhere near the wedding and just assumed it wasn't his scene. I vowed to make a better attempt to know the man after him doing this solid for me.

I jumped down from Olivia's truck just a few feet away from where Buck's beat-up little Nissan SUV was parked. The man had shit taste in cars but I got it, sometimes you just had to take the car you could afford instead of your dream car.

I didn't see any movement inside, but it was dark, so I leaned down and knocked on the back passenger window.

"Hello?"

Which was when I saw Mr. and Mrs. Winston sitting up ramrod straight in the backseat, duct tape not only over their mouths, but wrapped around their entire faces and heads.

I started to screech and jump backward. What the fuck??

"Don't worry, I got you," came Buck's familiar voice, and I relaxed, but only for an instant, because the second I looked over my shoulder, I knew something was wrong. Which was confirmed when Buck finished his sentence. "I got you. I finally got you all to myself, little Ruthie. And no one's going to show up to stop me this time."

18

Jeremiah

I waited until my brother and Charlie came back out of the house and rejoined the party before pulling him aside. I'd been seething the entire ceremony. I didn't know if I was more pissed at Reece or Ruth —him for putting me in this position and getting in between me and Ruth when we'd had something—no, I shook my head. It was better it self-imploded now rather than later.

We'd both just been running too high on insane sexual chemistry and overflow wedding pheromones. All of it was surface and based on a lie. Reece was only marrying Charlie so quick because of the baby.

Although… I had to admit, the way my little brother looked at his bride during the ceremony when they repeated the vows after Xavier… I shook my head. It didn't matter if my brother had found the real thing. Love.

What mattered was the lies. It was all based on a lie. And him being impetuous. Which always led to disaster. Sure, it all smelled rosy and looked beautiful now. But who was gonna have to pick up the pieces when everything blew the fuck up, huh?

Cheery band music played in the distance as I stood cross-armed outside the house. Finally the door cracked and I straightened as Reece looked out as if checking for the all-clear. When he saw it was just me, a look of relief crossed his face.

"The in-laws aren't anywhere around, are they? I've finally got Charlie back in a celebrating mood and her stomach's settled. I don't want anyone else ruining her day."

My arms went back across my chest. Oh, he was gonna pretend to be Mr. Responsible now? Mr. Protective Caretaker?

Where was this guy when he shoulda been putting on a rubber however many months ago? Nowhere, because my brother was all about whatever got him his jollies right there, right then. And now he was a husband and about to become a father?

"You and me need to talk," I stated, and his demeanor changed because he could tell I meant business.

He pulled the door tighter behind him to block Charlie, calling over his shoulder. "Just a few more minutes, babe. I'll be right back. No, nothing's wrong. Just keep resting. I'll come get you in a few."

Then he stepped out to join me and shut the door behind him.

"All right. Fine. It's been a long time coming," he said, glaring at me. "Let me have it."

I was a little taken aback. Usually when it was time to school my brother, he stood back and took it.

"Actually, you know what?" he said, shaking his head. "No. I'm fucking fed up with your high and mighty bullshit. You being born a few minutes early doesn't actually make you older. We're the same fucking age. I'm a grown ass man and I'm tired of your judgmental bullshit. My wife knows enough to tell off her parents when they're trying to get into our life when it's none of their business and brother, I'm ready to do the same to you."

"It's not the same at all. I took *care* of you when—"

"Did you? 'Cause the way I remember it, we took care of each other."

I scoffed. "You have no fucking idea the shit I did for you."

He threw his arms out. "Because you won't tell me! You think you're so high and mighty but you don't even know how to communicate. Being with Charlie has taught me what actual grown-up relationships look like and brother, I can finally see that *you're* still the child. We were never taught how to talk about shit, much less how to heal from all the trauma—"

I scoffed again and started to turn away when he grabbed my shoulder. I yanked away but he just got in front of me.

"Yes, fucking *trauma*. The way we grew up, that was fucking traumatic. We fucking survived and that makes us survivors. But you don't just go through that shit and come out normal. You have to deal with it. You can't just keep ignoring it. You have to talk about it, work through it—"

"I work just fine," I said through gritted teeth.

It was his turn to scoff. "Oh, that's what you call whatever the fuck it is you're doing?"

"What the hell is that supposed to mean?"

"Stomping through life, gruff and grumpy as hell? Pushing anyone away before they can ever get too close? You think that's *healthy*? Shit, if I wasn't so forgiving, you would have pushed me away too."

I stared at him. I wanted to punch him to get him to shut the fuck up.

But he just kept going. "For example, what the hell is going on with you and Ruth? Anyone with eyes in their heads can see you have feelings for the woman."

"She's moving."

He registered surprise and I remembered she hadn't told anyone else yet.

"And she lied to me."

"About what?"

"You getting Charlie pregnant."

He looked at me like I was nuts. "You mean she was loyal to her friend and kept a secret Charlie asked her to?"

He shook his head. "I'd ask what the fuck is wrong with you, but I know. Brother, both of us created this story where you were the one of the two of us who had their shit together, but that was a lie. You were just better at shoving it down deep. I think I was the healthier one all along because I could react to shit. I could show my emotions. You just shoved it all down so fucking deep and never let anyone else in. But it's not better. You aren't some fucking paragon. I'm sorry, brother, but you aren't. You were always just as fucked up as me."

I stood there, in the uncomfortable situation of being the one schooled.

I wanted to argue. I wanted to tell him to go fuck himself.

But all I really wanted was to go find Ruth, grab her to me tight, and never fucking let go.

Come to think of it, that was a great fucking idea.

I clapped my brother on the shoulder. "Good talk. Congratulations on the coming kid. You married an amazing woman and I think you just might be a great dad."

He looked surprised. "So... we're good?"

I nodded. "We're good."

"Oh. Well, great."

Then I turned and went to find my own woman. God knew I hated to admit when I was wrong, but I wasn't so much of a jackass that I couldn't see it when I was being hit in the face with the truth. And Reece was always excellent for that.

So, yes, I was an ass and it was time to find my woman, tell her that, and beg for her forgiveness.

Except she was nowhere to be found.

I caught up with Olivia near the bar, flirting with some hick looking motherfucker. "Hey, Liv, you seen Ruth?"

She shook her head. "But I can call her." She pulled out her phone from her purse. Right. I shoulda thought of that.

But her brows furrowed at something she saw on the phone.

The band started up some song that had the crowd cheering so that I missed what Olivia said next.

"What?" I shouted and she turned the phone so that I could see a message. It was from Ruth.

Ruth: borrowing your car to get check from the Winstons. Buck stalled them on way to airport so I could catch up. Be back soon!

My eyes searched out the time tag. It had been sent almost two hours ago. I messaged back from Olivia's phone in case Ruth was still mad at me and blocking my calls. How long till you're back?

And then waited impatiently. No response.

I looked back at Olivia. "She should be back by now, yeah?"

Olivia shrugged, leaning close to shout over the music. "Yeah, it's less than an hour to the airport from here, so even if she went all the way there and back…"

I frowned and handed her the phone. "Find me if she texts back."

I pulled out my own phone as I walked away toward my truck, dialing Ruth's number. Why the hell would *Buck* of all people have offered to drive Charlie's parents back to the airport. Well, if they offered to pay him, I bet he would. But if they were paying, then why would he be stalling so Ruth could catch up?

I wish she'd offered more damn information in the text. I saw Reece and Charlie rejoining the guests. Good. At least they could recoup the rest of the wedding and get memories of their special day that wouldn't be tainted by that witch of a mother-in-law.

I hoped she wasn't giving my Ruth trouble now.

My Ruth.

Dammit, it was true. I'd thought of her as mine for…a while now. I was jealous of that fucking job because it took her away from me. Even having her live all the way in Austin was interminable because she wasn't under the same roof as me. And now she was going to move to Fort Worth?

Not if I could help it.

I didn't bother telling Reece where I was going. He'd had enough of me for one day. He had his bride to look after and I still wanted him to be able to salvage some of his wedding day without thinking an iota more about his in-laws. If they were giving Ruth any trouble, I'd deal with it without ever involving him.

And I'd tell Ruth what a giant fucking idiot I was. I hurried around to where all the vehicles were parked, pulled out my keys, and hopped in the truck.

Before I pulled out onto the gravel road leading to the side trail that led to town, I looked at my phone and clicked on the GPS app.

I'd cloned Ruth's phone a long while back, after the tornado. I'd done it with everyone's phone—Reece and Charlie too. After Charlie's bastard of an ex showed back up—then his best friend a week later, blustering and blowing smoke about foul play—well, I wasn't going to take chances when it came to my family. Ruth was Charlie's best friend, and Charlie was my brother's girl, i.e., she was family. That was what I told myself, anyway.

But now I knew as I clicked on the button that tracked her phone and felt a bone-deep relief that I could see exactly where she was, it had always been more than that. I'd needed to know she was safe not because she was Charlie's friend. I'd needed it for me. And good thing, too, because her little dot wasn't flashing anywhere *near* the airport.

I zoomed in on the phone and frowned. Why the hell was she out near Five-Mile Dam? And then, just like that, the dot disappeared. The fuck?

I clicked the button for her phone again, but nothing.

An error message appeared when I clicked for more information. Error: Device has been turned off or lost signal.

"Dammit," I said, throwing the truck into gear and peeling out.

Maybe she'd just decided to go take a rest at the Dam instead of coming back to the wedding after she'd taken Charlie's parents to the airport? In the dark?

Maybe she was avoiding *me*.

But still, Five-Mile? It was a swimming hole in summer. There was nothing to do there this time of year. It wasn't exactly a hiking spot.

Whatever. I'd get there and we could finally have it out, once and for all. I'd put all my cards on the table, or try to.

Reece's words echoed in my head: *You were always just as fucked up as me.* Could I admit that to Ruth and explain that I needed her? That I wasn't as perfect as I always pretended, even if it was hard for me to swallow my pride and fucking admit it. There were reasons I was the way I was and maybe someday I'd even be able to open up and talk about it...

In the meantime, I just shoved the truck into fifth gear and opened up the engine as I sped down the back streets of the hill country as the sunset streaked across the sky.

Twenty minutes later, the sun had dipped below the horizon and the pinks and oranges were settling into the purple haze of twilight as I pulled into the Five-Mile parking lot.

I drove from one end of the parking lot to another, my car lights on bright. But nowhere did I see Olivia's little Honda.

Goddammit, I'd seen Ruth's phone lighting up right near this spot less than half an hour ago. Where the hell was she?

Had I missed her on the road somewhere or had she already moved on? But when I pulled out my phone to see if I could catch her GPS dot, *I* couldn't get any signal. "Fucking great," I muttered, shoving my phone back onto its holder in the dash as I spun the truck around and pulled out of the driveway onto the backroads again. I drove a little ways down the stretch of road in the direction I hadn't come from and slowed when I saw a vehicle pulled off and parked on a slight inlet a little way down from the dam.

I came to a stop and squinted at the car. It wasn't Olivia's car but it looked familiar. Then I caught sight of the gold naked woman emblem on the back of his mudflaps.

Holy shit. It was *Buck's* car.

I was shoving out the door of my truck even as I tried to figure out what the *hell* Ruth would be doing out here in the middle of nowhere with Buck of all people. They never interacted that much, as far as I knew.

Then again, maybe she had *really* wanted to get back at me. Or wash me out of her system. The best way to get over one man was to get under another one, some bullshit like that.

One part of me knew I couldn't blame her after everything I'd said and done, while another, less evolved part of me wanted to find Buck and leave him without any teeth for daring to touch what was mine.

Not knowing what I'd do once I found them together, I couldn't stop myself from stomping forwards toward the SUV and yanking open the door.

Only to find no one inside. The raging bull in my chest was only slightly mollified. Because I realized a moment later that just because I hadn't found them in flagrante in the car didn't mean they weren't curled up somewhere else cozy nearby.

I turned on my phone's flashlight and looked around in the increasing darkness. At first, I didn't see anything but the normal Texas scrub brush that lined the sides of all Central Texas sideroads… until in the distance, I glimpsed a small structure. A storage hut of some kind? An old bathroom for Five-Mile Dam Park before it had become the lost, forgotten place it was now until folks remembered it each summer when the water levels rose enough to make it of interest again?

I lowered my flashlight and stomped toward the place. How had they even gotten inside? And Jesus, I knew Ruth was adventurous, but coming out here in the middle of nowhere to fuck *Buck* of all guys? I wasn't usually judgmental when it came to my coworkers, but Buck was by far the weakest link at the farm, happy to slack off work whenever he could. And the way he spoke about women… well, yeah, I was surprised Ruth would dally with him no matter how pissed I'd made her.

Brambles pulled at my slacks and I barely dodged a large cactus as I made my way toward the structure. Getting closer didn't help me figure out what it was meant to be used for any better.

But I did see a door, cracked a little, and I could see light pouring out from within.

They were in there.

I swallowed hard.

A bigger man would have turned around right there and gotten back in his truck. But I wasn't a bigger man. I needed to see for myself, even though the image would torture me.

So I pushed open the door.

And realized that yet again, I'd been a complete fucking idiot who had completely underestimated the situation I was in.

Because as I opened the door to the most fucking horrific scene of Ruth struggling uselessly, duct-taped to a chair, the Winstons unconscious or worse on the ground, the unmistakable feeling of a gun barrel pressed to the back of my neck.

"Step inside and don't make a single fucking noise," Buck's voice came so close I could smell his alcohol-soured breath from behind me. In fact, the fucker smelled so bad, he must have intentionally been standing downwind. These Texas boys grew up hunting and tracking. How long had he been stalking me? Ever since I got out of my truck, stomping around and flashing my presence like the big dumb bastard that I was.

"Okay," I said, lifting my hands up in the air. "Not sure what I'm walking into here, Buck, but I'm sure we can work something out."

"Shut the fuck *up*," Buck said, digging the barrel of the gun more painfully into the back of my neck until I took a step forward into the small hut. Which looked uncannily like something out of Dexter's wet dreams, apart from the fact that it was missing plastic spread out everywhere. But I couldn't tell if the two elderly folks on the ground were even breathing. I wasn't a fan of Charlie's mom and dad or anything, but I hadn't wanted them *dead*.

"Ruth?" I asked. "You okay?"

She just looked at me with wide eyes like, *are you kidding*? Fair point.

"On your knees!" Buck shouted from behind me.

I stayed standing, not moving an inch. "So you can execute me? I don't think so. Let's just take a second and talk this thru. Is it money you're looking for? Cause I'm worth a lot more than Ruth here. In fact, if you let her go and keep me, this would all be a lot more easy to handle. One hostage instead of three, it'll be a breeze. And Xavier, my employer, is wealthy. He's like a father to me and he'll pay if you just—"

And then I turned and tried to yank the gun out of his hands. I was taller and larger than Buck, and physically superior. But the bastard must have been on his guard. He pulled the trigger and even though I was able to yank the gun up so the shot landed in the ceiling instead of my forehead, all my focus was on the gun.

I didn't even see him pull out the needle until he'd shoved the shot into my thigh and depressed the plunger, right as I knocked the gun out of his hands.

I started to scramble after it, but only made it one single step before crumpling to my knees.

Ruth's muffled screams against the duct-tape at her mouth were the last thing I heard before the world went dark.

19

Ruth

I couldn't believe this was happening. It was already so horrible, being caught and manhandled by *Buck* of all people, him babbling at me the whole time between taking swigs from a seemingly endless supply of beer bottles from a cooler he kept in the foot of the passenger side footwell of his truck—babbling about how I'd ruined his life.

His driving had been terrible and I had the slimmest hope that a cop would pull us over for reckless driving. But he was taking backroads, not the highway. I'd felt another hope rise when I heard the sound of another truck and the rustle of someone outside.

But Buck had just put his finger to his lips, grinned maniacally at me, and then slipped out of the cabin.

The next thing I knew, Jeremiah—*Jeremiah,* of all people! How had he found me? What was he doing here?—had somehow appeared at the door. I'd tried to scream and warn him but it was too late.

Then there was that brief second where he'd even managed to get the gun away from Buck!

But in the end, none of it mattered. I recognized the packaging of the sedative Buck had yanked the syringe out of. It was for the damn *cattle*, and I had no idea how much he'd used on the Winstons or Jeremiah, or if they could possibly survive it.

And now I was left alone again, with a psychotic Buck, breathing hard as he looked down at Jeremiah, slumped on the floor beneath him.

"Take *that*," Buck said, kicking Jeremiah hard in the lower back. I screamed uselessly into the tape gagging my mouth.

"What?" Buck said, looking over at me. "You got somethin' to say? All this is your fault. None of 'em would even be in this if it wasn't for you."

I went still and swallowed, then nodded and looked down, then bowed my head before finally looking back up at him.

He stared at me for a moment, unsure, before asking, "I take that tape off, you gonna start screamin'? Because no one can hear you out here. This bastard's the only one dumb enough to come looking for you in the middle of the night on this stretch of road. Though how the fuck did he find us?" Then he frowned and came toward me, feeling all down the folds in my puffy dress until his hand landed on my phone. He looked at it in disgust, walking around behind me and shoving my finger against the little pad to unlock it. "Did you manage to send a text for help, you little bitch?"

I shook my head back and forth rapidly as he came back around to the front of me, finger tapping through the apps on my phone.

He came over, grabbed the tape at the corner of my mouth with his dirty-fingernailed hand, and ripped it off in one swift go.

"Who else did you text, bitch?" he yelled in my face.

"Ouch," I gasped, then sucked in a large breath of air through my mouth. Buck was so pungent I could all but taste him on the air—but also the cedar forest air around us. "No one," I gasped. "I didn't even text him." I nodded toward Jeremiah. "I don't know how he found me."

Buck turned around and reached into Jeremiah's pocket, pulling out his phone. He unlocked it the same way he had mine and then started laughing, looking up at me. "Loverboy was tracking you. Guess he knew you were a faithless little bitch."

Jeremiah had put a tracking app on my phone? When? Who the fuck cared? I tried to listen hard and could just make out the sound of rushing water, so we were near a river or a stream of some kind.

Not that that information helped narrow it down considering we were in Central Texas and you could barely throw a rock without hitting a stream or spring of one kind or another. Especially considering the rain we'd had lately. Even the usually dry creek beds would be running with water right now.

No, goddammit, it was official, I had no idea where Buck had taken me and less and less confidence with each passing moment that he'd told anyone where he was going or that I was even missing.

But maybe he'd told his brother where he was going?

Or… more likely, he'd just taken off like a goddamn cowboy all by himself to come find me.

And now here we both were. Trapped by this man who was clearly more than a crayon or two short of a boxset.

Buck glared at me, face only inches from mine. "So?" he demanded. "Don't you recognize me?"

I stared back at him incredulously. "Um, yeah. You're Buck. You've worked with me for—"

"NO!" He slammed the wooden wall behind my head, shaking the entire hut. "I said, *look* at me. Fucking *look*!"

I did. I looked. And saw the bloodshot eyes of a man who would have little problem doing violence to me or maybe any woman. I shook in my seat as he raised the gun toward my temple.

"Look!" he shouted again. "Don't you fucking see him? Our father? I have his fucking *eyebrows*." The hand with the gun swung wildly toward my face as his hands gestured with every word. So it took a second for what he'd said to sunk in.

But as soon as it did, it wasn't a surprise.

Of course my father had cheated on my mother. He'd been

unfaithful to his family in every other sense of the word, so of course in this most base and basic way he had been too. He'd not only cheated on my mother but fathered *children* with some other woman.

"Sister," Buck said, leaning in and smiling, his foul breath between us.

I jerked back from him, revolted by him, by everything he was saying.

"Don't want to hear that Daddy dearest fucked around on Mommy?" Buck sneered, backing away but only slightly. He was still bent over in my space, so close that when he spoke, his spittle landed on my cheeks. "Well, he did. And he told my mother that he'd leave yours and come and be with her. He told her that for years. Years and years we lived in a shit little apartment on the shit side of I35. All while you grew up *here*, in the hill country on your *ranch*, riding horses and being the belle of the redneck county motherfucking ball."

He waved his hands wildly, his steps unsteady as he paced back in the tiny space of the shed, smaller than ever with Jeremiah's big body on the floor.

"Daddy pays for college, for *everything* for his little angel, and what do *I* get? A child shot from the same cock? The same *blood*? I get a few cards over the years. Once, in junior high, I came home and caught him fucking my mom in the kitchen. Before he left, he came by my bedroom and pulled out a couple twenties for me, like I was her pimp."

I winced, understanding how deep of a bastard my father was now. Some small part of me had always hoped there was some sort of redeeming quality in him deep down… and I do mean *way* deep down, because he was a fucking asshole on the surface. But no, this just confirmed what had always been my lived experience of the man.

"I'm so sorry he did that to you, Buck. He was a terrible person. Believe me, growing up with him was no gem, either—"

"Don't you dare, you little fucking bitch!" he screamed with renewed energy, the gun rising back to my temple with alarming alacrity. "You think we're going to stand around sharing oh our poor daddy stories?" He laughed caustically.

"When Mama was too washed up for him to keep coming around, he ignored us completely. And when Mama died, and I came to your house, and I knocked on your door, shivering, starving, begging for help so I didn't go into the system, begging for my own *father* to take me in, when I was barely fourteen years old, do you know what that man did?"

I shook my head and then whispered, "No. I don't know what he did. You know I don't."

"That's right," he said with a bitter smile. "You don't. Because he was so concerned with you and his wife not knowing of my existence that he drew me to him in what I thought was a hug. But it was really only so he could turn me around to hide my body with his and cover my mouth and nose with his hand. And then he pulled one arm behind my back and perp-walked me out past the corner lot until we were covered by the neighbor's fencing."

I sucked in a huge rush of breath. "I'm so sorry. Did he at least—"

"He told me if I ever came within a hundred feet of him again, he'd get a restraining order against my ass. But if I disappeared forever, he'd give me a thousand dollars. Right there, on the spot. No matter what, though," Buck laughed caustically, "he said as he shook me hard, would there be no further contact between us. Daddy didn't have no son."

Buck pulled his gun from the holster at his hip and traced the barrel down my cheek. His voice went darker, more serious. "Only his precious *daughter* got to bear his name. And so when he died, of course his ranch went only to her. Only everything for *her*."

"Buck," I breathed out, "it breaks my heart hearing that—"

"Oh, I'll break your heart," he said, and punched me in the gut. I coughed in pain and writhed over in half as far as the restraints would allow. Oh *God*, that hurt. "But maybe I'll start with your lungs."

I heaved for breath as I looked back up at him. This man who shared a father with me. My *brother*. We shared the twisted DNA of that man and this was what could become of it. Or maybe it was the way he was nurtured, maybe our father's hatred and rejection had made him this way.

I'd have to deal with the mixed feelings of realizing that my father, who I'd always understood to have hated women, preferring me when he'd had a son of his very own to run the business… But then again, maybe my dad's ego was such that he would have found fault no matter who his progeny were, because apparently neither of us was enough of a reflection of himself or his values. Not me, who fit into his world, from his perfect but otherwise barren wife, to his son, who was a boy but born from a mistress, and overly surly to boot.

But I couldn't think of any of that right now. I had to be smart. Strategic. Obviously trying to empathize with him wasn't going to work. But maybe I could appeal to him in other ways.

"So what's the plan here, brother?" I asked, making my voice monotone and staring him in the eye. "You want to kill me, but what are you going to do with them?" I nodded toward the three people on the floor. "What do Jeremiah or Charlie's parents have to do with this? Be smart. You need an escape plan."

He laughed in my face. "Escape? I'm not the one tied to a chair, bitch."

I tilted my head to the side. "No, but even if you kill me, kill all of us, where do you go next? You need money, Buck. You never got what you deserved, isn't that what all of this is about? Dad screwed you over. But you can still make it right."

His hand came to my throat and he squeezed. "Shut the fuck up! There's nothing left of Dad's money. You said so yourself."

I nodded, feeling my eyes bulging as he squeezed my windpipe off. I was only trying to stall for time, but what if I only pissed him off and made him kill me quicker? Shit. Oh shit, I couldn't breathe!

But he finally let go of my throat and I gasped for air as he demanded, "*Talk.*"

"You're right," I finally said, my voice raspy from being choked. "But *they* do." I nodded back toward the floor, this time at the Winstons. "They have a lot of money. And they'll pay up for him. He wasn't wrong about that. But only if they're alive and able to pay the ransom."

Buck frowned, and I could tell his alcohol-befuddled brain was struggling to follow the logic of what I was saying.

"They're rich," I said, offering what I hoped were the magic words. "I mean, really, really rich. You stumbled into a jackpot and didn't even know it."

He reached for his gun again and raised it back toward me. "You better not be trying to trick me."

I shook my head vigorously. "You saw the wedding they were paying for and the clothes they wear. Check the label on her jacket. It's Chanel, and not a knock off. All you have to do is go drop them somewhere with instructions on how to pay you. And they've been unconscious the whole time so they won't know how to trace you back here. Just think," I said, rushing now that I saw he was considering my words. "You could get everything you always deserved and then be over the border to Mexico before anyone even realized what was going on. You'll live like a king there."

He was imagining the life I was picturing for him; I could see it on his face. Then he looked back down at the floor at the two older folks, then to Jeremiah.

"What if they don't pay?"

"They'll pay."

He glared back at me. "What if they don't?"

I swallowed. "Then you do whatever you were already planning to do with us."

He smiled at that. A slow, cruel smile. "Who says I won't even if they do pay?"

I let him see the tremble in my lip, and it wasn't just for show. He might be drunk and not too bright, but he was also unstable and violent. He was completely unpredictable and I had no idea what he might do next, if he'd listen to what I was suggesting or slug me in the stomach again.

But then, as the seconds ticked interminably by, he finally shoved his gun back into the holster at his side and leaned down. He grabbed

Mrs. Winston roughly by her arms and kicked the door to the shed open. He started dragging her out the same way he'd dragged her in. I winced at how painful it looked but she was still completely knocked out, limp as a stuffed doll as her body bumped ruthlessly over the wooden step at the door's threshold.

I stared at Jeremiah, willing him to move, to twitch—*anything*—but he stayed as still as stone for the five minutes it took Buck to get Mrs. Winston to the car and come back for Mr. Winston.

Mr. Winston wasn't quite as inert as his wife, though. Was he starting to wake up from the tranquilizer? He groaned and his eyelids fluttered when he hit the same sharp wooden step at the doorway. Buck paused, but when Mr. Winston immediately fell silent again, he continued to drag the slight man over the punishing, uneven ground.

I closed my eyes. I wanted to start squirming and immediately start fighting my bonds. But no. *Be patient. Just be patient. He's almost gone.*

I waited to hear the engine in Buck's shitty little truck start up, straining to listen. I was straining so hard to hear faraway sounds that when the door to the cabin slammed open again, I jolted in surprise.

It was still just Buck, naturally. He had his fat roll of duct tape in hand, naturally. He leaned down and yanked Jeremiah's hands behind his back, rolling him roughly onto his stomach in the process. Around and around he rolled the tape until Jeremiah's wrists were secure behind his back. Buck did the same thing to Jeremiah's ankles. Only once he'd used a significant amount of tape did he stand up and wipe his brow. He turned and glared at me, the only expression his face seemed capable of making.

"Don't move a single fucking muscle. I'll be right back."

I nodded obediently, but that didn't stop him from coming toward me with the duct tape roll in hand. He ripped off a piece and resecured it over my mouth before turning and walking out the door.

A little while later, I finally heard the sound of a truck starting and driving away.

Only then did I slump in my bonds and breathe out for what felt like the first time in hours.

"*Ereiah*," I tried to scream Jeremiah's name through the stupid tape on my mouth, wriggling and writhing against the bonds at my wrist and ankles. Of course he didn't look up. Mr. Winston had been dosed several hours ago and only now had he started to stir.

Buck had tied tape around my chest and arms too, but if I could just get my wrists free... The tape was tied so tightly, I couldn't even twist my arm in the tight loop of tape. Dammit. All the twisting just made it feel *tighter*. I swore into the gag at my mouth.

Over and over and over, I fought against my bindings, and swore, and fought some more... and swore some more. The whole time, I felt a ticking clock over my head. How far away would Buck go to dump out the Winstons. He'd go far if he was smart. Then again, it was Buck we were talking about.

Then again, he had managed to stay under the radar all this time. Dammit, why hadn't I been paying attention to my creep radar when it came to Buck? I'd always felt there was something slightly... *off* about him. But if Reece and Jeremiah trusted him, so could I. Or so went my logic whenever my spidey senses tingled about Buck. Whenever I bothered thinking about him, which frankly, I just hadn't bothered to do very often.

But apparently, the whole time he'd been obsessing about me.

Because, oh my God, was it him who'd been sabotaging the fences all last year before the tornado, back when I'd still been living at the ranch? And my car? The sugar in the tank? It had to be him. How long had he been planning this and what exactly *was* this?

That Buck didn't intend for me to make it out alive seemed clear.

I struggled even harder against my bindings, rocking the chair back and forth on the plywood floor of the shed.

I stopped just before I knocked the chair all the way over. Fat tears sprang out of my eyes even as I was furious at them. Now was no time for crying. I had to get us the hell *out* of here while Buck was gone.

I had no delusions about the Winstons actually paying ransom for Jeremiah or me. I'd just wanted to get Buck the hell out of here, to stall for time so I could try to escape or for someone else to find us.

The more I tried to wriggle free, though, the more helpless the situation felt. It wasn't as if I had something sharp like they did in the movies to cut the tape with. The more I twisted against it, the more the tape bunched up and became even more ropelike. Goddamned duct tape. I'd seen specials where people built *boats* out of this crap. It was impenetrable.

Oh God, oh God, what if I couldn't get free? What if all of this had been for nothing? I'd refused to let myself think about it, but now it seemed more and more certain that Buck would drop off the Winstons, then come back and enjoy finishing off every revenge fantasy he'd cooked up over the years.

My breaths became short, huffing too fast out of my nose since my mouth was covered and I jerked in my chair, rocking it but not caring, too panicked in my need to get free. I had to get out of here. I had to get free and go for help, I had to—

Oh shit!

I'd rocked the chair too hard and I'd tipped it just like I was afraid of and then I was falling, falling over sideways, right toward Jeremiah—

I crashed into the floor with a jolting, "*Oof.*" And landed half on top of Jeremiah in the small space.

Not that he even twitched, he was still knocked out cold. And unlike in the movies, my wooden chair hadn't shattered on impact or anything helpful like that. Nope, I was still just as trapped, but now I was sideways on the floor, my head on Jeremiah's chest.

I bowed my head into his warmth as his huge chest moved up and down rhythmically in his unnatural sleep.

And unable to do anything else, I let the tears flow.

20

JEREMIAH

No. Fuck no. *I couldn't be back here.* I'd escaped. I'd escaped and gotten me and Reece as fucking far away from here as quickly as humanly possible.

So why couldn't I move?

I heard her voice, *their* voices, in my head. Always in my head. I was blindfolded on the bed. She'd wanted it that way and though I'd been uncomfortable with the idea, I'd agreed.

It was just supposed to be one night.

What was one stupid night of my life compared to me and Reece's future? It was no contest. Reece had been at death's door when I dropped him off at the shelter earlier tonight. They'd only had space for one more so I pushed him inside and ran.

And then hit the streets the way so many of our peers did.

Enough. It was all fucking enough. Me and Reece had gone to the streets to escape the foster system, but we'd turned eighteen four months ago. It was time to get us the fuck outta here.

But to do that, we needed money. And more than we'd get from a good Saturday juggling or picking pockets at the park.

My jaw flexed as I sorted through possibilities.

The solution was obvious.

If I was honest with myself, I always knew it would come down to this. A shudder went through my body the more I thought about it. Then I hiked up my backpack and held my head high. I wasn't going to sit here and wallow in my sad little life like a damn baby.

I lifted an arm over my head in a futile attempt to protect myself from the rain and then started jogging in the direction of Polk Street.

The jog didn't do much to warm me up since all my clothes were soaked through. I saw a few other figures dotted up and down the street when I got to Polk. They all stood on the sidewalk near the curb.

Hawking their wares.

Their bodies.

Most of the other street kids Reece and I knew did it. They talked about their 'clients' like it was no big deal. And it wasn't really. Not compared to another night of seeing Reece suffering, sick, and never knowing if we'd have a roof over our heads for the night or not.

I hesitated only one more moment before dropping my backpack, then pulling my jacket off and tying it around my waist. My soaked shirt was molded to my chest. I ran a quick hand through my hair.

I hadn't had a proper shower in a few weeks but me and Reece were far more conscientious about personal hygiene than most of our fellow unhoused. I always made sure we had a stick of deodorant between us and we sponged down every time we had access to a bathroom.

I looked up and down the road. Cars continually drove past but none slowed down. It was only around eight o'clock. Maybe too early for this sort of thing.

I rocked back and forth on my toes, shoving my hands in my jeans pocket. Christ, was I supposed to do something other than stand here? Was there some secret wave I should make at the passing drivers to let them know I was open for business? How the fuck did this work?

But just as I was thinking that, a beat-up gold-toned Buick with peeling paint slowed down and pulled over in front of where I was standing.

I peered at the car, taking a step forward. Between the darkness and the drizzling rain, I couldn't make out the driver. Were they just looking for a parking spot or—

The passenger side window rolled down and I cringed when I saw the face that emerged. The driver was leaning over to peer at me. He was a red-faced guy with about three chins and a case of adult acne. He looked me up and down in a way that made my stomach queasy.

"Fifty to blow me," the guy said.

I backed away, hands up. "Hey man, I'm not into that." It was just an impulse response. I wasn't stupid. I knew most of the pickups here were dudes looking for... but no. Just no. Not my first time.

The guy scowled at me. "Fuck you." The car wheels screeched as he pulled back into traffic.

"Hey. You."

I looked behind me and saw a couple guys headed my direction.

"Yeah, you. Who you think you are, crashing our spot?"

Shit. One of the guys was as skinny as me, but the other one was thick around the middle, with wide shoulders. The last thing I needed was to end up with a broken nose or worse, in the hospital.

Maybe this was a bad fucking idea. Especially just jumping in like this. I should have gone to Star or one of our other friends and asked them to show me the ropes. But fuck, I didn't want to deal with any goddamn pimps. I just needed to get a little bit of cash and—

"What? You fuckin' deaf? I said, who you think you are, motherfucker?" The big guy pulled something out of his pocket. Holy shit, was that a knife?

I backed away from the approaching men. Just as I did, a beamer slowed down by the sidewalk in front of me.

Screw it. Even if it was another troll, the situation was getting way too fucking hot here. I ran for the car, jerking the back door open and jumping in before yanking it shut behind me.

I was greeted by two surprised faces looking back at me from the front seat. A man and woman, both who looked to be in their late thirties. They were dressed up—the guy in a suit and the woman in a black cocktail dress. Neither was stunning, but they weren't ugly either. Just plain old regular folks. Well, maybe not so regular considering they were trolling Polk Street looking for a prostitute.

"Hey," I said, giving an awkward wave. "So, uh, we can discuss terms while we drive?" I glanced anxiously out the window. The two guys had paused a few feet away, looking unsure how to proceed. I didn't plan on waiting for them to figure it out. "You don't want to stay parked in this neighborhood. There are gangs. They'll yank you out of your car to steal it." It was an exaggeration. That kind of thing didn't usually happen but I'd say anything to get the car moving.

The man let out a nervous, "Oh," and reached down to punch a door lock button. "Okay. Well, let's go then."

He put the car in gear and then we were driving. I breathed out a sigh of relief.

"So, um," the man cleared his throat. "What are your rates? To, um, you know. Spend the night?"

I glanced between him and the back of the woman's head. Apart from the first glance at him, she'd been sitting ramrod straight in the passenger's seat. I was sitting directly behind her so I couldn't see more than the back of her head. Her thick brown hair was twisted in some kind of fancy knot. As I looked, though, I caught her watching me in her visor mirror. She quickly averted her eyes.

Okay. So these two didn't exactly seem experienced with this whole thing. Or were they just playing that way? You never knew what people's kinks were. That was something else I'd seen far too much of. I might only be eighteen but me and Reece both had some experience. Orgasms were one thing that felt good no matter who you were or what your living situation was. I was just religious about using protection.

"So I'll be fucking both of you or just one?" I tried to clarify.

"Um," the guy said, his voice stuttering. "Well, it's Victoria's birthday and I told her she could have whatever she wanted. And she's always had this fantasy, so…"

I looked the guy up and down. The suit looked expensive. And the car certainly wasn't a cheap ride. These two had dough. And I needed enough for two bus tickets East.

"Five hundred for the whole night." I tried to make my voice confident even though inside I was kicking myself as soon as it was out of my mouth. Shit. They were going to toss me out on my ass for asking too much. No way would they pay that mu—

"Done," the woman said, her voice soft and breathy.

Oh. Wow. "Deal," I said before they could change their mind. "Cash up front."

"Done."

I hadn't had a clue when I smiled in relief and sank back against the seat and ten minutes later followed them up to their penthouse apartment that I was voluntarily walking into hell, or that "Victoria" was the goddamned devil herself.

My eyes jerked open and my breath stuttered to find I wasn't in Victoria's nightmare of a *playroom*, but somewhere small and dark and musty, with a weight on my chest and my hands—

My wrists were tied painfully tight behind my back.

Fuck!

I blinked drowsy, heavy eyes, struggling to figure out what the *fuck* was going on. Everything felt heavy, even as a familiar panic raced through my blood.

How had she found me? The first thing I'd done as soon as I'd gotten free of her was find Reece and then get on a bus and run as far away from San Francisco as I could get—

The weight on my chest moved and I tried to lift my head to look down. Oh fuck, my head was a thousand pounds, I could barely lift it an inch off the ground, barely lift my eyes open.

And what I saw made no sense.

Ruth. Ruth, tied to a chair that had been knocked over sideways on top of me. It was dark, but moonlight came in from a high window. Enough so I could see tape over her mouth. And I could feel her wriggling and hear her inaudible noises as she tried to say something even though the tape muffled her words.

I blinked again, even though each time it felt like lifting a mountain.

Ruth.

I was here with Ruth.

Ruth.

The wedding. We were at the wedding, and I'd proposed to Ruth, and she'd said yes. But then, then something had happened—

I shut my eyes, trying to concentrate and recall.

And then it all hit with a flood. The wedding. Charlie's mom figuring out she was pregnant. Me being an asshole and my brother calling me out on it.

Going after Ruth and finding—

Oh shit!

My eyes popped back open. I'd followed the tracker I'd put on Ruth's phone, because after what had happened to me so long ago, I'd always been hypervigilant. I knew the evil people were capable of, no matter how happy-go-lucky my twin was, how good he wanted to believe humanity was.

I knew better. So I put a tracker on everyone I loved.

And I loved Ruth.

The second I'd stepped in the door and seen her tied up, my heart had sunk through the floor, but like a fucking idiot, I hadn't gone on alert fast enough and someone had gotten the drop on me.

Judging by how goddamned drowsy I felt, they'd used some powerful shit too.

It felt like it took every ounce of strength to move my head from side to side to check out the room and evaluate the situation.

A shed, we were in a small shed. More memories hit. Me walking toward the shed. The small, out of the way swimming hole at the little dam.

And how I hadn't told a fucking soul where I was going.

Like a total goddamned idiot. Of course I hadn't expected this, but hikers never expected to get lost either. They still told people where they were going. It was a basic of going into a situation where unexpected things could happen. Reece and I always had a hard and fast rule that we never went anywhere without letting the other know. Especially after Victoria. I was worse than ever.

But that had been back when we were street kids and over the years, my brother had used the line about being tired of having his brother as his keeper too many times over the years so I'd eased up.

This was bad.

Very bad.

I had to get us out of here.

Because after being handcuffed to Victoria's bed for two months straight, only allowed out on a leash to use the bathroom and for "walks" on a treadmill, also while leashed, I'd finally escaped, and swore I'd never, *ever* allow myself to be so powerless again.

I pulled at my wrists and felt the tug. Not cuffs. I looked at how Ruth was tied to the chair.

Duct tape.

Buck had likely used the same thing to tie me up.

A glance down at my ankles confirmed it.

His first mistake.

I looked around. Speaking of, where was the fuckwad? I opened my mouth, which tasted as dry as if it had been stuffed with cotton balls. Swallowing didn't help, but I did it several times anyway and then tried again, croaking out a low, "Where?"

Moonlight glinted off Ruth's wide, tear-reddened eyes as she looked toward the door and shrugged.

Did that mean she didn't know? Or that he could be returning any minute? Fuck. Neither was good news.

I tried to roll my body to the side but barely shifted. Goddammit, *no*. If Buck was psycho enough to lock us up here like this, he'd probably do much worse when he got back from wherever the hell he'd run off to. He'd brought Ruth to a secondary location and that was always bad news. I'd had reason and opportunity to study this shit extensively. It rarely turned out well.

I sucked in several quick short breaths and huffed them out just as fast. I forced myself to think of just how much danger we were in.

And then I did the one thing I knew would throw my body into a panic and adrenaline response. The one thing I usually fought at all costs.

I intentionally thought about Victoria.

I thought about how her "husband"—really just a favorite slave of the moment—had held me face down on the bed while Victoria put the handcuffs on.

I relived how Victoria took her time with me that first night, introducing me to a kind of pain I'd never known before, and also forcing me to pleasure, over and over.

Over the next weeks, she'd use me in every way imaginable—a toy for her pleasure and a toy to torment because she was a sadist in every sense of the word.

By the middle of the second month, I was half convinced I loved her. Just like the other slaves she brought in and out.

Except that they all consented to be there.

I didn't.

Which was why I was her favorite to play with. The more I begged for her to let me go, the more she loved to play with me.

By the end, I just wanted to die. I barely remembered who I was.

But Reece.

I never forgot my brother. Flesh of my flesh. The brother with my face.

She broke me down so far that I lost my sense of self, that I could almost forget my life… but I could never forget him.

Every time I looked in a mirror, I saw him. He was the one thing she couldn't steal.

I grunted in fury, adrenaline bursting in every cell as I rocked my body again. I expected to rocket to a sitting position with the energy of my anger. The fury and rage at what Victoria had done to me, the way she'd made me doubt my own sanity, sexuality, *everything*—

But I only rolled a little. Still, it was enough to dislodge Ruth from my chest.

Fuck, it *hurt* to move. It was so fucking difficult. My body felt like it weighed a thousand pounds. Two thousand pounds even.

But I thought of my rage at Victoria, of how helpless I'd felt those months of nights, knowing she'd come home and torment me into the long hours of morning. And I roared inside my head and forced my muscles to contract and move again.

This time I managed to heave myself up onto my knees. I swayed drunkenly, but at least my body was upright, my arms tight behind my back.

I breathed out and fought to stay upright. I knew what I needed to do, I just needed to stay conscious to do it. But fuck, the idea of getting all the way to my feet seemed nigh impossible at the moment.

I looked down at Ruth, though, and realized I didn't have only anger to fuel me.

Like back then, it wasn't just anger that had kept that last wall of sanity up, safe from Victoria's total influence and control.

It was love, goddammit.

Love for my brother, and now this new love. Love for Ruth. The woman I wanted to make mine forever.

But I could only do that if I saved her from this hell hole.

I roared again and leaning one shoulder against the side of the shed for balance, heaved myself up on one knee, and then, without letting myself stop this time, continued pushing until I was on my feet.

Ruth made encouraging noises from where she laid sideways in her chair on the floor. I didn't dare look down. I was barely keeping steady. My head swam crazily and the world tilted even as I got my second foot underneath me. I leaned my whole body against the wall when my knees buckled and threatened to dump me back on the floor. No, goddammit, *NO*.

I gritted my teeth and forced my knees to lock, keeping me up.

But getting up was only the first part of this trial. I sucked in a deep breath, and before I lost focus, lifted my arms as high as I could behind my back, then brought them down hard against my tailbone.

Nothing happened.

I hadn't been able to produce enough force. While in my mind the movement had been dramatic, in reality, I'd done little more than lift and drop my arms a few inches or so. That wouldn't do jack shit, though. For this to work, I needed momentum and *force*. I'd watched enough YouTube videos on escape techniques to know that.

So I bent over, leaning my shoulder against the wall so I didn't fall, and lifted my arms again until it was painful—this one needed to count—and then I yanked my arms back down as hard as I could, imagining I was smashing Buck's face in.

The duct tape around my wrists split down the center, right along the seam in the tape like when you ripped a piece off—a critical weakness that few would-be abductors realized. You could do the same with zip-ties. Enough force and they'd snap the same way, at the seam.

And then I crumpled to the floor, all my energy momentarily spent.

Ruth cried out in alarm. I didn't have much energy to tell her I was okay, but when I brought my arms out from around my back and crawled over to her, her eyes were wide and excited. I pulled the tape off her mouth first.

"Get my hands," she said. "Then I can help you with the rest."

I didn't bother wasting the energy to nod, I just got to work heaving my million-pound arms around to tug at the tape binding her. It took longer than I would have preferred, but finally I'd gotten her wrists free and together, we pulled her hands and arms free of the tape.

I fell back and rested, breathing hard as she made quick work of the tape around her ankles and then mine.

"Okay, that was badass," she said. "And now it's time to get the hell out of here. Come on."

She held a hand down to me, and then, quickly realizing that wasn't enough, she leaned down and put her shoulder underneath my arm. Which was a ridiculous idea considering how small she was.

I wasn't a skinny street kid anymore. I'd bulked up to be twice the size I was as an eighteen-year-old, and there was no way Ruth was dragging me out of here without assistance.

So, as exhausted as I was, I pushed for a little bit more adrenaline and got to my knees, then stumbled to my feet, Ruth attempting in vain to steady me.

I'd just reached out for the wall when we heard the sound of a truck engine pulling to a stop nearby.

Ruth's head snapped my way, eyes wide and terrified. "It's him. He's back."

Well, shit.

21

Ruth

"Get behind me," Jeremiah whispered fervently.

Hilarious. He could barely stand on his own two feet.

But there was no time to argue. Or make a plan. Or do much of anything. I looked around the shed that was frustratingly empty other than the chair.

Buck had a *gun*. And he was crazy.

All we had on our side was surprise. If only Jer had woken fifteen minutes earlier we might have gotten the hell *out* of here.

But I knew well enough that wishes never did anyone good. And my heart raced as I gave another panicked look up at Jer when we heard footsteps approaching.

Fuck.

So I didn't stop to think.

I separated myself from Jeremiah and he tried to move between me and the door, as if he thought I was actually giving into his suggestion of letting him take on Buck by himself.

Men.

I shook my head and hurried to grab the chair from the floor, quietly so as to not ruin our one advantage.

And then when the door rattled and finally opened, I flipped the chair so that I held the legs, the back out like a battering ram. And then I screamed like a banshee, surprising the hell out of both Jeremiah and Buck, and ran straight at Buck, straight through the door, ramming the chair into him and plowing into him just as he reached for his gun.

The ringing of a gunshot exploded through the air.

22

Jeremiah

I wasn't quick enough to save her. Oh God. Oh God oh God.

I've failed her just like I was always so terrified I'd fail my little brother. We were always so cold and wet, huddling against buildings and over vents in the sidewalks where hot air would pipe out of the San Francisco streets. But you had to fight for those spots and it didn't matter anyway during the long, interminably rainy days some winters, temperatures just above freezing.

And here I was in the dark and the cold again.

And Ruth—

Ruth!

I struggled to get up, to go to her—

But it was dark. So dark. And I couldn't move. Why couldn't I move?

I tried to call out to her. I tried to scream. But the darkness only closed in deeper, taking me back.

Swallowing me down the throat of the night and into its belly. I choked and screamed as I tried to open my eyes, to claw my way out. But I couldn't move. Couldn't move because she had me trapped.

And then I was afraid that I'd never left. I'd never left that fifteen by fifteen foot room dungeon. I'd never escaped to Texas with my brother. I'd never met Xavier, or made it to Mel's ranch.

I'd never met Ruth, who challenged me and frustrated me and made me feel more alive than I'd ever known was possible.

That had all been the mirage. The dream.

I'd been in the dungeon all this time, only escaping where my mind would take me. Dreaming up a whole life.

And now it had come to an end.

Ruth was gone. The ranch I'd fought so hard to make solvent with my brother—gone. None of it had ever been real.

And now I didn't want to open my eyes because I knew I'd only see her horrible, taunting face, and she'd break me down until I begged, and beg I would. I'd beg and snivel and be less than a man, less than a beast under her whip—

Are you going to be a good dog today? Victoria would always ask when she came in. And I would hurriedly crawl as far as my leash would allow so I could lick her boots and show that yes, yes I would be very a good dog that day. So that maybe, just maybe, I would get fed.

Ruth! I screamed, even though I knew it would earn me a beating, even though I knew another woman's name on my tongue would infuriate her.

Predictably, I felt the tug on my leash.

And then I frowned.

The tug wasn't coming from the leash around my neck.

The tug was at my hand.

And more than a tug it was a squeeze. But the squeeze was so tight. So tight, a hand holding mine.

Victoria had never once held my hand.

Why couldn't I open my eyes? Had she blindfolded me? She did sometimes, but usually only during what she called 'scenes.'

I struggled again to open my eyes. And realized I couldn't open them because they weighed a thousand pounds. My whole body wasn't right.

What was going on?

Nothing made sense.

Where was I? It didn't smell right. Nothing was right, nothing was—

I cracked my eyes the tiniest bit and glaring bright light flooded in, causing me to immediately close them again.

And God, my side hurt. Fuck, it fucking *hurt*. How had I only just now registered it?

Noise too, there was noise all around me, though it sounded like it was coming through a long tunnel, distorted. Like a bunch of voices were all talking over one another.

And then someone yanked my eyelid open and shined a light in it.

I winced back and the voices got louder. What fresh hell was this? Some sort of medical play Victoria had cooked up with her twisted followers?

"Mr. Walker? Mr. Walker? Can you hear me? Do you know what day it is?"

I blinked or tried to, my eyes crusty, and finally opened them against the light again. Where I was met by a man in a lab coat looking down at me very seriously.

"Mr. Walker, you've been involved in an incident. I'm going to check out your vitals quickly."

I shook my head, still struggling to understand what was happening.

I opened my mouth and tried to ask, but only a croak came out of my desert dry throat.

"Shh, don't try to talk," said the man dressed as a doctor. He looked toward the side of the room. "Nurse, can you get him some water. And then let the family know he's awake?"

Family? Was this really a hospital and not some twisted setup of Victoria's?

The nurse he'd spoken to, a round woman in her late fifties, came forward with a cup and helped fit the straw in my mouth while the doctor kept talking.

"A bullet was lodged in your abdomen, causing a severe intraperitoneal hemorrhage as well as damage to your liver and intestines. We managed to stop the bleeding just in time and did surgery to repair your damaged liver, and then put you in an induced coma to heal. But two days later you developed peritonitis and we thought we might lose you all over again. In short, you're a very lucky young man."

A bullet? What the hell was he talking about?

I awkwardly sucked on the straw, dribbling some down my chin, which the nurse wiped away. I felt like a damn child. I struggled to clear my throat. "Ruth?"

Then I blinked. Reece. I'd meant to ask for Reece, my brother.

But as soon as her name came out of my mouth, I remembered. Not everything—but I remembered I'd gone after her. And then something...something bad had happened.

"Ruth?" I asked again, more urgently, frantic almost. I tried to sit up but was barely able to, my energy was so drained. And the pain in my abdomen roared at the attempt.

"No, no, sit back," the doctor urged, grabbing my shoulder and pushing me back down. "Nurse, go get his brother."

I watched the nurse hurry out of the room helplessly. "Ruth," I managed again before my head collapsed back on the pillow.

I felt woozy, like I was about to pass out again, when I heard voices.

The door opened. "I told you, I'm his fiancée, goddammit. I don't care if visiting hours are over. He was shot because of me and you are letting me in there. Reece, *tell her.*"

I knew that voice. A rush of relief so hard hit me that I didn't fight the goddamn tears that suddenly filled my eyes. She was here. She was safe. Nothing else mattered. I didn't care how the fuck we'd gotten here.

I heard the harsh slapping of bootheels against linoleum, a quick *bang bang bang bang,* and then her scent was surrounding me.

Ruth. She hugged my neck and I inhaled her.

Oh my God. Oh fuck. It had all been real.

She was real and she was here and we were safe.

She pulled back long enough to look me in the eyes, our foreheads touching. I met her hazel eyes, still blurry and confused about all that brought us here. But I knew what I wanted, forever and ever.

So I got it across in as few words as possible to spare my still sore throat: "Let's elope."

Her worry turned to laughter as she covered my face with kisses.

EPILOGUE

Ruth

"So we just did that," I giggled, throwing my arms around my husband's neck as he backed me into our Vegas hotel room two and a half months later.

"You bet your ass we just did, Mrs. Walker," Jeremiah said as he shoved me up against the wall, kicking the door shut with his foot and bracing his hands on the wall on either side of my head. "And now I intend to consummate the vows we just made before Elvis so you know I damn well mean it."

He plucked the cheap little tiara with attached veil out of my hair and then dug his fingers in, dragging my head back. He followed with his mouth, missing my lips and latching onto my throat instead.

Oh God, *yes*.

The past two months had been incredible. Maybe that was mean to say, because the physical therapy and rehab Jer had gone through hadn't always been easy. It was only last week he'd been able to get on a horse again and walk more than a couple blocks without getting winded.

It hadn't mattered, or maybe it had allowed us to connect on an even deeper level intimacy wise.

He'd finally let me in. He told me things he'd never told anyone else, not even Reece. He told me about what happened to him when he was desperate on the streets, how he was essentially kidnapped and held captive by that evil bitch, how he barely escaped. How when kids like him disappeared, no one ever went looking.

No wonder he had a hard time letting anyone close, or ever letting down his walls. At first he was monotone as he told it all to me, but by the end, he'd broken down weeping, burying his face in my breasts. Like a child in need of comfort from the mother who had never been there for him.

And I'd held him so close and whispered to him that I had him, that I loved him, and that I'd never let anything bad happen to him ever again. A foolish promise to make but one I was still determined to bring true. This precious man was everything to me. He'd been so strong for so long and I wanted him to know that now he could put down that heavy burden. He could lay it down now and rest in my arms.

But Jeremiah never was one to rest for long, or to allow himself to be out of control. And I understood better than ever after he gave me his deepest secrets.

So I gave myself to him with a trust *I'd* never been able to give to anyone before. Because Buck's revelations about my father had freed me from the man's legacy. I wouldn't allow that man or his opinions of me to torture me any longer. He no longer had any control over me.

Look what his mind games had done to his other child.

Buck was in prison now and would be for a long time. The Winston's lawyers would see to that. They hadn't taken kindly to being kidnapped and extorted. Plus the attempted murder charge for Jeremiah. No, he wouldn't see the light of day for a long, long time. Good fucking riddance. He might be my half-brother but he'd effectively squashed any sisterly sentiment I might have ever felt. In the end all he'd ever proved was that yes, he was his father's son.

And now Jeremiah and I were free.

I kissed him back just as vigorously as his leg slid between mine. He angled himself in such a way that I could feel his hard cock through his slacks, right at my center. I groaned, already so turned on from seeing his love-filled eyes during the cheesy ceremony downstairs. It hadn't mattered that I was holding plastic flowers or that the chapel smelled like hairspray and cheap perfume.

It was perfect. I was finally uniting with the man of my dreams. The man I wanted to spend the rest of my life with. Ours would never be a conventional life. We fell in love during someone else's wedding celebrations, cemented our affair while stranded in a storm, to this day had sex more often out of bed than in it—being married by an Elvis impersonator felt just about right.

"I want you wet," Jeremiah growled to me as he reached up underneath my simple skirt, shoved my panties aside, and palmed my pussy.

I shuddered against his hand, my forehead falling against his chest as I began to shudder. I was so ready for him. So *beyond* ready for him—

"I'm wet," I whispered, unnecessarily, since he could feel just how wet I was.

But he shook his head, still strumming a spot that had me almost sputtering, it was so goddamn good.

With his other hand he began tugging at my shirt. I got the idea and helped him pull it off over my head.

I wasn't wearing a bra. I figured when in Vegas...

His dark eyes flashed when he saw my tits spring out. My pussy throbbed at the look on his face and I whined in need.

He grinned then, a wolf's grin. Dear God, how was I ever going to survive the night?

Because apparently my new husband had plans for me. Plans that began with getting me in the shower. Since that's where he led me next, one hand buried in my pussy the whole way.

The second he flipped on the light in the bathroom, I gasped. He'd obviously splurged on the room because the shower was *huge*. It had several rain showerheads, along with a built-in bench. All in a rich marble.

He let go of me briefly to set the water to steaming and I whined with the loss of contact. He already had me in a sort of trance and we'd barely begun. But as soon as he'd gotten the water going, he began stripping down.

My mouth dropped open as I watched him reveal inch after inch of hard muscle. Working the ranch morning to night day after day had sculpted him into a god.

I reached out, longing to run my fingers down his six-pack abs. He was naked all except for his black boxers that were stretched obscenely in the front from his hard cock.

He caught my wrists before I could reach out and make contact, though. "Ah ah ah," he warned. "Only good girls get rewarded. Are you going to be a good girl tonight, Mrs. Walker?"

I looked up into his eyes and nodded fervently, biting my lip in the way I knew drove him crazy. "I'll be such a good girl," I whispered, batting my eyes at him.

He groaned in the low way I knew meant I was driving him to the brink and my sex pulsed again. He yanked me close, shoving down my skirt and panties and all but hauling me into the shower with him.

The hot water was a shocking sensation that, with my body already primed, had me spasming and clutching onto Jeremiah.

But he was so keyed into my every emotion and reaction, he was ready for me, and again grasped my wrists before I could close around him.

He held my right wrist in a firm, commanding grip that had me shuddering in front of him as the steamy water soaked me from behind. He lifted my arm up and placed my palm on the wall, pressing it lightly there in a way I knew meant I was to leave it there. When he released my wrist, I kept my arm raised and palm to the wall.

He did the same with the other wrist, so that I was grasping the top of the frame for the opaque glass shower door, spreading me so that I might as well be tied to an invisible St. Andrews Cross. As if he had the same image in mind, he nudged my feet open wider so that I was completely exposed to him. Completely vulnerable to whatever he might want to do to me.

All the while the water steamed the air around us and dripped down my body, lighting up every nerve ending in ways I'd never realized they could be awakened.

"Close your eyes and feel me," he whispered.

I obeyed. I'd learned when he wanted to be in control, it was best to give in and go for the ride. I trusted him to never let me drop. I *trusted* him, something I never thought I'd be able to say of any man. But he had earned it, over and over again.

So I closed my eyes and when his fingertip began tracing the hot, wet skin at my wrist, slowly working his way to my inner elbow, and then down further to my bicep, to my underarm, sloping around to my breasts—

"Oh!" I gasped when he came to my nipple. He didn't grasp it or suck it... No, he just began to lightly flick it and tease it with his big, calloused fingers. Back and forth and then forth and back again. Just that one point of contract on my body.

I squirmed where I stood as an orgasm built. Jesus Christ. Was he really going to make me come from simply flicking my nipple?

But the more he teased, gently and then harder and harder, and then soft again so I was whining and twisting where I stood, ready to beg, arching my chest out toward him and squirming until finally, *finally*, he gave in and dipped his head to clamp his lips on me and sucked.

I cried out in relief and the pleasure that stroked through my sternum and down to my pussy at the pressure of his tongue on my nipple. Jesus Christ, when he did it like that, it felt like my nipple was a second clit. Yes, yes, just like that. Right there, oh, oh God—

I arched my back, thrusting my breast harder into his face and just then I felt his teeth against my nipple, biting—

I screamed, not caring who heard, not caring about anything but the insane connection between me and the man ministering so perfectly at my nipple.

And yet, as perfect as that felt—

"I need you," I whined, even as I still rode the high he'd just taken me on. "Please. Please, fuck me. I need you inside me. I want you so deep inside—"

I barely got the words out of my mouth before he had me hefted against the wall again, just like he had when we'd first walked in the door.

Except this time there was no fabric between us. And when he reached down and positioned his cock at my center, all I felt was thrilled anticipation for what was to come. I couldn't get him inside me fast enough.

"I'm gonna put my arms around you," I said breathlessly.

Still, I waited until he gave a little harsh nod before dropping my hands from where he'd placed them earlier.

This was our compromise when it came to sex. He'd begun to allow me to touch him; he just asked me to warn him so it didn't hit him out of the blue and he could give himself a second to prepare for it. I knew it was so huge and just another step in the magic that was us. I suspected I wasn't the only feeling some healing from our union and I wasn't the only one who'd noticed it. Just last week Reece had stopped me, kind of amazed at the change he'd seen in his brother.

Still, I didn't take anything for granted and I was slow and careful as I placed my arms around my new husband's neck, watching his face to make sure the sensation didn't take him anywhere bad in his head.

But his eyes were locked on mine and he seemed fully present as he shifted us so that the steaming water fell between our chests, creating a pool there. And then he leaned me against the marbled wall of the shower and reached down for my leg, lingering to palm and squeeze my ass before hiking my leg up around his waist.

Which had the added benefit of notching his cock perfectly into position. I couldn't help the whining noise that came from my throat as I wiggled against his cock. It felt like torture not to have him inside me. Like I could feel the emptiness, the memory of his fullness like a ghost. I couldn't be truly satiated until—

Just the tip of him began to breech my pussy and already I began shuddering. He was so thick that as he pushed in, he strummed several spots that had me squirming for friction already. And he was only in maybe half an inch.

"Don't tease me," I said throatily. "I'm not above begging. Please, please, Jer, fuck me. Oh God, please fuck me—"

One of his thick hands landed roughly on my hip as he pulled out a little, then thrust back in, creating the most amazing friction.

I did a full body roll at the action and then he was filling me. Oh God he was filling me. So deep. Then deeper still. I opened to him and clenched around his cock for dear life.

"I can feel every inch of you," I gasped.

"Fuck, honey," he said, teeth clenched, "so can I. You feel like fucking silk."

He pulled out and then thrust back in. "Like a fucking silk vice. This is where I've wanted to be all day. But I wanted you as my wife first. I wanted to fuck you as your husband. I wanted to claim you," he thrust in, then pulled out again, "and fill you," he thrust back in, all the way, all the way deep, hitting a spot so deep I spasmed and clenched my legs around his ass, arching my chest into his.

He leaned in and slurped the shower-water off of my collarbone. And then he kept sucking, and sucking, and there was so much sensation all at once—him so thick and deep inside me, the body-shuddering melt of his lips suckling my neck, and steam and water on my skin.

My head fell back as I came, quaking and clenching around his cock.

"Fuck," he broke from my neck to hiss, and then he stood up straighter, cementing his body against mine and the wall as he began to fuck me in earnest. I was shuddering putty beneath him, coming harder and longer with his every thrust.

The more I clenched on him, the more intense my orgasm, and I could see from the look of agonized pleasure on his face that it felt good to him, too, so good.

"Honey," he gritted out. "Oh fuck, *honey*."

"Yes," was all I could get out, surprised I could manage actual human words at all. "Yes, yes, *yessssssssss*."

He came with a roar, his hands palming my cheeks and pressing his forehead to mine, a communion deeper even than kissing.

And as we both stood there huffing for breath in the steamy aftermath he whispered a single word, "Mine."

Nothing would ever wipe the smile off my face that word elicited. "Yours," I whispered back. "Forever."

His eyes flashed open, dark and possessive. "You better fucking believe it, *wife*," he said before devouring me in a long kiss.

And I felt a rupture of joy in my chest, because this was only the beginning.

∽

WANT MORE STEAMY ROMANCE FROM STASIA BLACK?
Keep reading for a sneak peek of Theirs to Protect, book one in the Marriage Raffle Series...

THEIRS TO PROTECT SNEAK PEEK

PROLOGUE
AUDREY

"And do you, Audrey Dawson, accept the five men before you as your wedded husbands, for as long as you all shall live?"

Audrey's entire body shook as she looked around the front of the church at the men who had been strangers only three weeks before. She didn't know them much better now. God, was she really going through with this?

Yes. You already decided you would. No turning back now.

So she stood up straight and forced her voice not to waver as she said, "I do."

Nix, the biggest and scariest of all of them, leaned forward and kissed her knuckles before sliding a delicate gold band onto her fourth finger.

Oh God oh God oh God.

"Clan Hale is born today," the pastor announced triumphantly. "Six are united as one. What has been joined today let no man tear asunder!"

The crowd cheered and Audrey looked at the little church,

packed mostly with men, women dotting the crowd only here and there.

"You may now kiss your bride."

Audrey felt her eyes pop wide open as she looked between her new husbands. Would they line up or something? Was this more of a ceremonial thing, like just a quick peck, or—

Clark, the handsomest of the five, stepped up, wrapped one arm around her waist and dug his other hand in the back of her hair.

And then he kissed the living daylights out of her.

His tongue wasn't forceful. It was teasing. Coaxing even. She gasped in surprise when he grabbed her and he'd used the opportunity to sneak his tongue in her mouth. It wasn't thrusting, though.

No, he teased just the very tip of it against hers in a way that had her gasping in shock. Because holy *crap*. She'd never known that her tongue was a direct conduit to— to— Down *there*.

By the time Clark pulled back, he had to steady her on her feet. He'd literally kissed her wobbly. She was gasping for breath and immediately lifted her hand to her mouth, blinking in confusion.

Well. That answered her question about whether the kiss was ceremonial or not.

Next stepped up husband number two, Graham. His cheeks were pink and his gaze was slightly off to the left, like usual, not quite meeting her gaze. Unlike Clark, he just dropped a quick kiss to her lips before pulling back. Okay, good. She didn't think her heart could take another Clark style kiss at the moment.

Then came Danny. Sweet, teddy bear Danny. Her eyes widened as he approached, though. His face was full of excitement, but he was coming at her with his tongue already half out of his mouth. Like a hungry dog panting for a meal. She was about to pull back in alarm but Clark grabbed Danny's arm and pulled him away before he could reach her. "Nope."

"Wait, what?" Danny exclaimed. "You can't do that. It's not official till I kiss her!"

"Not until I've sat you down and explained a little more bit about the birds and the bees, my boy. And how the hell to kiss a woman."

"But—" Danny whined.

"It's all right," Audrey laughed nervously. Okay, so she wasn't the only one who had no idea what the hell she was doing. She stepped forward impulsively and landed a quick peck on Danny's lips. When she pulled back he looked totally dumbstruck. Like she'd just revealed she'd cured him of an incurable disease, not given him a brief little peck on the lips.

Then was Mateo. He looked as pale and scared as Audrey felt and her heart melted. Mateo had been special from the beginning. Where Nix was constantly demanding, Mateo only wanted to give. To serve. To see to her every comfort and desire.

She felt a kinship with him she couldn't explain. Maybe because she could tell he'd experienced loss too. Not in the same way, perhaps, but he'd suffered. Deeply.

And in spite of her circumstances, Audrey couldn't help but want to give back to him. So when he stepped up to her, body trembling even more than hers had been throughout the wedding ceremony, she was the one who reached for him.

She lifted her head and pressed her lips to his. Tentatively at first. But then she remembered the way Clark had moved his tongue and so she experimented. She ran her tongue along the seam of his lips and he inhaled sharply. Feeling a little bolder, she cupped his face and deepened the kiss.

And it was sweet. Very sweet. Mateo's body melted against hers. He pulled her closer and she could feel his racing heartbeat through his chest. His tongue moved and started to dance with hers and it wasn't long before again, she was breathless and dizzy with the sensations being awakened in her body.

When she finally pulled away, the warmth pulsing out from her center was so shocking, for a moment she just stood there, frozen.

Not for long though, because Nix was apparently impatient for his turn.

He grasped her around her waist and all but dragged her up and into him. And his lips weren't gentle or teasing or coaxing.

They were demanding.

Devouring.

She gasped for air and it was his breath she was breathing in. He seemed determined to imprint his lips on hers.

Oh— *oh*—

He sucked her tongue into his mouth and it—

Her entire body shuddered against him. Oh God, was it possible to have an orgasm just from a *kiss*?

How was he doing that— She didn't even like him, so why was she— Oh, oh *God*—

She groaned into his mouth and he kissed her even deeper, though she wouldn't have thought that was possible. He swallowed her gasp, his hard body pressing into her soft one. He reached up and dug his fingers into her hair, ignoring the pins and cradling the back of her head so he could kiss her even more deeply still.

And she abandoned herself to it. She didn't mean to. God knew she didn't mean to. But he was— It was—

When he finally dragged his mouth away, she barely stopped herself from whimpering in disappointment.

It took her several moments to realize there were whistles and catcalls coming from all around them.

Because they were standing at the front of a church.

Oh God.

Embarrassment hit hot and blinding.

How had she lost control of herself so completely? She felt her cheeks flame.

"Time to take our wife home," Nix declared.

Then Nix was all but dragging her out the back of the church, the rest of her husbands—oh God, her *husbands, plural*—following on their heels.

But apparently she wasn't moving fast enough for Nix's liking because the next thing she knew, he'd hoisted her up and over his shoulder like he was a damn caveman and she was his most recent kill.

"Nix!" she called out, smacking at his back. It wasn't her fault she couldn't walk at his breakneck speed. Unless she literally wanted to break her neck. Whoever had invented high heels back before The Fall needed to die. Maybe with a high heel impaled in his neck. Those things were death traps. Why did women used to subject themselves to them?

On the other hand, maybe this was better. After several jarring steps, she closed her eyes and clung to Nix's back. Just go loose, go along with what the guys had planned.

She would not hyperventilate. She would not hyperventilate.

So she was about to lose her virginity.

In a fivesome.

No big deal.

She just had to lay there. Right?

…

Who the fuck was she kidding?

It was a big deal. It was a huge, giant fucking deal. But she'd told herself she was doing it tonight and it was a promise she meant to keep.

Before she knew it, and far before she was ready—because who was she kidding, she wasn't sure she'd ever be ready for this—she was being deposited on the bed.

Five men.

Her.

And one very large bed.

Apparently there wouldn't be any waiting to consummate this marriage.

∾

Find out what happens when Audrey, a girl lost and alone, stumbles into a town that requires all women to enter into a Marriage Raffle. Is Audrey really ready to take on Nix and his clan?

One-click Theirs to Protect now so you don't miss a thing!
https://geni.us/Th2Pr-EN-n

Want to read an EXCLUSIVE, FREE novella, Indecent: a Taboo Proposal, that is available ONLY to my newsletter subscribers, along with news about upcoming releases, sales, exclusive giveaways, and more?

Get Indecent: a Taboo Proposal
https://geni.us/SBA-nw-cont

When Mia's boyfriend takes her out to her favorite restaurant on their six-year anniversary, she's expecting one kind of proposal. What she didn't expect was her boyfriend's longtime rival, Vaughn McBride, to show up and make a completely different sort of offer: all her boyfriend's debts will be wiped clear. The price?

One night with her.

ALSO BY STASIA BLACK

Sci-fi Romances

Draci Alien Series

My Alien's Obsession [https://geni.us/MyAlOb-EN-w]

My Alien's Baby [https://geni.us/MyAlBa-EN-w]

My Alien's Beast [https://geni.us/MyAlBe-EN-w]

Marriage Raffle Series

Theirs To Protect [https://geni.us/Th2Pr-EN-w]

Theirs To Pleasure [https://geni.us/Th2Pl-EN-w]

Theirs To Wed [https://geni.us/Th2We-EN-w]

Theirs To Defy [https://geni.us/Th2De-EN-w]

Theirs To Ransom [https://geni.us/Th2Ra-EN-w]

Marriage Raffle Boxset Part 1 [https://geni.us/MaRaBx-EN-w]

Marriage Raffle Boxset Part 2 [https://geni.us/MaRaBx-2-EN-w]

Freebie

Their Honeymoon [https://BookHip.com/QHCQDM]

Dark Contemporary Romances

Breaking Belles Series

Elegant Sins [https://geni.us/ElSi-EN-w]

Beautiful Lies [https://geni.us/BeLi-EN-w]

Opulent Obsession [https://geni.us/OpOb-EN-w]

Inherited Malice [https://geni.us/InMa-EN-w]

Delicate Revenge [https://geni.us/DeRe-EN]

Lavish Corruption

Dark Mafia Series

Innocence [https://geni.us/Innocence-EN-w]

Awakening [https://geni.us/Awakening-EN-w]

Queen of the Underworld [https://geni.us/QuOfThUn-EN-w]

The Innocence Trilogy [https://geni.us/InBx-EN-w]

Beauty and the Rose Series

Beauty's Beast [https://geni.us/BeBe-EN-w]

Beauty and the Thorns [https://geni.us/BeNThTh-EN-w]

Beauty and the Rose [https://geni.us/BeNThRo-EN-w]

Billionaire's Captive [https://geni.us/BiCa-EN-w]

Love So Dark Duology

Cut So Deep [https://geni.us/CuSDe-EN-w]

Break So Soft [https://geni.us/BrSSo-EN-w]

Love So Dark [https://geni.us/LoSDa-EN-w]

Stud Ranch Series

The Virgin and the Beast [https://geni.us/ThViNThBe-EN-w]

Hunter [https://geni.us/Hunter-EN-w]

The Virgin Next Door [https://geni.us/ThViNeDo-EN-w]

Reece [https://geni.us/Reece-EN-w]

Jeremiah [https://geni.us/Jeremiah-EN-w]

Taboo Series

Daddy's Sweet Girl [https://geni.us/DaSwGi-EN-w]

Hurt So Good [https://geni.us/HuSGo-EN-w]

Taboo: a Dark Romance Boxset Collection [https://geni.us/Taboo_Bx-EN-w]

Vasiliev Bratva Series

Without Remorse [https://geni.us/WiRe-EN-w]

Freebie

Indecent: A Taboo Proposal [https://geni.us/SBA-nw-cont-w]

ABOUT THE AUTHOR

STASIA BLACK grew up in Texas, recently spent a freezing five-year stint in Minnesota, and now is happily planted in sunny California, which she will never, ever leave.

She loves writing, reading, listening to podcasts, and has recently taken up biking after a twenty-year sabbatical (and has the bumps and bruises to prove it). She lives with her own personal cheerleader, aka, her handsome husband, and their teenage son. Wow. Typing that makes her feel old. And writing about herself in the third person makes her feel a little like a nutjob, but ahem! Where were we?

Stasia's drawn to romantic stories that don't take the easy way out. She wants to see beneath people's veneer and poke into their dark places, their twisted motives, and their deepest desires. Basically, she wants to create characters that make readers alternately laugh, cry ugly tears, want to toss their kindles across the room, and then declare they have a new FBB (forever book boyfriend).

∽

Join Stasia's Facebook Group for Readers for access to deleted scenes, to chat with me and other fans and also get access to exclusive giveaways:

Stasia's Facebook Reader Group: https://www.facebook.com/groups/1047415562052038/

∽

Want to read an EXCLUSIVE, FREE novella, Indecent: a Taboo Proposal, that is available ONLY to my newsletter subscribers, along with news about upcoming releases, sales, exclusive giveaways, and more?

Get **Indecent: a Taboo Proposal**
   https://geni.us/SBA-nw-cont-w

When Mia's boyfriend takes her out to her favorite restaurant on their six-year anniversary, she's expecting one kind of proposal. What she didn't expect was her boyfriend's longtime rival, Vaughn McBride, to show up and make a completely different sort of offer: all her boyfriend's debts will be wiped clear. The price?

One night with her.

∼

Website: stasiablack.com
Facebook: facebook.com/StasiaBlackAuthor
Twitter: twitter.com/stasiawritesmut
Instagram: instagram.com/stasiablackauthor
Goodreads: goodreads.com/stasiablack
BookBub: bookbub.com/authors/stasia-black

facebook.com/StasiaBlackAuthor
twitter.com/stasiawritesmut
instagram.com/stasiablackauthor
amazon.com/Stasia-Black/e/B01MY5PIUH
bookbub.com/authors/stasia-black
goodreads.com/stasiablack

Printed in Great Britain
by Amazon